SIDELINE BLUES
by Wil

Series by MAUREEN HOLOHAN

A
MINSTREL®
BOOK

Published by POCKET BOOKS

New York   London   Toronto   Sydney   Singapore

A MINSTREL PAPERBACK *Original*

A Minstrel Book published by
POCKET BOOKS, a division of Simon & Schuster, Inc.
1230 Avenue of the Americas, New York, NY 10020

Copyright © 1998, 2001 by Maureen Holohan

ISBN: 0-7434-0745-8

First Minstrel Books printing August 2001

10 9 8 7 6 5 4 3 2 1

A MINSTREL BOOK and colophon are registered trademarks of Simon & Schuster, Inc.

Front cover illustration by Doron Ben-Ami

Printed in the U.S.A.

This book is dedicated
to those who live, learn,
and love like Wil.

You have no limits.

Chapter 1

When I was a kid, I ruled in gym class.
But soon my days of glory came to pass.
In my mind I had a perfect physique,
which I felt made me rather unique.
I was a fine athlete who loved to compete,
yet my coaches thought I was far from elite.
Teachers told me to stick to the books.
But from the first day I played sports, I was
   hooked.
Although my dad had never seen me play,
I knew my mother in heaven watched me every day.
I hung out with a group of girls who loved to play ball,
during the winter, spring, summer, and fall.
Angel, P., Ro and Mo have kept your eyes on the
   page.
Now it's time for Wil to take the stage.

The Broadway Ballplayers

*T*hump! I stood up and rubbed my burning forearms. Without hesitation, Anita Kaplan lined up and drilled another volleyball right at me. As the ball flew through the air, I set my powerful legs, then swung my muscular arms. In a flash the white blur ricocheted in the wrong direction again. I glared around at the rest of my teammates, and all I received were a few encouraging claps.

"You've got it!"

"Shake it off!"

My eyes stopped on Anita, and I panicked as she slammed another shot at me. I braced myself, but the ball slapped against my arms like a belly hitting the surface of a pool. I winced in pain and shook my wrists. *Come on! That's not fair. You're hitting it way too hard!*

"Get your body under it, Wil!" Coach Kim yelled at me.

On the next serve I got my body under it all right. When the ball thumped me right in the chest, I crashed down to the ground and gasped for air.

"Are you okay, Wil?" Penny Harris asked.

Tears began to fill my eyes. *Be tough, Wil. Be tough!* Penny, who was one of my best friends, always cheered me on. I couldn't let her down. "Yeah," I moaned as I pulled myself up. "I'll make it."

"Let's go, Wil!" Coach Kim hollered. "Be ready this time!"

Oh, puh-leze! Of course I was ready. I adjusted my glasses and danced around in my spot. I held my breath as the ball came sailing over the net. I swung, accidentally shut my eyes, and missed.

2

"I've had enough!" Coach Kim called out. "Penny, step in for Wil."

What? So I had a few bad plays. I'll get the next one.

"Penny!" Coach Kim yelled.

Penny jumped to my spot on the floor.

"Don't sweat it, Wil," she whispered to me. "You'll get the next one."

I threw my hands up in the air and moved off to the side. When Anita wound up for the next serve, I leaped back on the court in front of Penny and smacked the stupid little ball. *Thump!* It was a perfect soft bump right to our setter.

I stared at my coach as I wiped my hands off. *Now how come I'm not starting?*

"Get a drink, Wil," Coach Kim ordered.

I strutted off the court, feeling bigger and badder than any player out there. Then I glanced at the clock. Thirty-three minutes and twenty seconds until our eighteenth practice of the year was over. I walked to the water fountain and took a long drink. As I closed my eyes and enjoyed the rest, I felt a tap on my shoulder.

"Hurry up!" Molly "Mo" O'Malley complained.

I took my time.

"This is your last warning," she said firmly.

I began slurping the cold, refreshing water.

Molly, who had never fully grasped the concept of patience, huffed and yelled loudly, "What does it take for a girl to get a drink around here?"

With my head still over the water fountain, a sharp elbow dug into my side. I sent one of my fierce elbows right back at my friend. "A lot more than that!"

Molly gladly accepted my challenge. We both laughed hard as we jostled for a spot in front of the fountain.

"Wil and Molly!" Coach Kim hollered. "Five laps and fifty sit-ups!"

We both groaned.

"But, Coach Kim—" I pleaded.

"No *buts!*" she shot back with an evil glare. *But* was her least favorite word, and unfortunately, most of my replies began with it. I looked at Molly, clicked my tongue against my teeth, and said, "Thanks a lot!"

"Well, if you weren't hogging all the water!" Molly replied.

"Move it!" Coach Kim screamed.

Penny looked at the both of us and shook her head. She grinned and then returned to the drills. Penny Harris performed almost flawlessly through every practice and every game in virtually every sport. As I dragged my tired, sore body next to Molly's, I recalled the good ol' days when I dominated the sports scene. Back in third and fourth grade, nobody could touch me or my huge biceps. In the third grade alone, I scored 525 baskets, hit 35 homeruns, and scored 101 goals. But during middle school, everybody caught up to me, and all I could do was hang on for the ride.

"Hurry up!" Molly muttered to me.

"Hey, Mo. Why are you always in such a hurry?" I asked.

Sweat poured down my head as if I had just stepped out of the shower. Once I started perspiring, there was no stopping the salty waterfall.

"How many more?" Molly gasped. We both carried

nice frames of muscle and additional padding in some areas. Even though I had been named after track star Wilma Rudolph, I unfortunately did not run like the amazing woman. The good news was that Molly didn't, either.

"One and a quarter laps," I said.

With one lap left, Molly burst into an impressive sprint. The thought of challenging her did not even cross my mind. When I finally crossed the spot where we had started, we both fell to the ground. Molly started pumping out sit-ups twice as fast as me.

"Slow down, Mo Muscles," I grumbled.

Molly ignored me. I grunted and groaned on every crunch. After a few seconds Molly stopped, panted for air, and turned to me.

"I lost track," she said.

"You've done twenty-one," I said with certainty.

"That's it?" she gasped. "No way!"

"Yep," I shot back.

Although some would have called it a lie, I simply divided Molly's number of sit-ups by two. Molly had actually finished 42. But I didn't want her to finish before I did. I still had 25 to go.

"How many have you done?" Molly asked.

"I'd prefer to keep that kind of information to myself, if you don't mind," I replied.

Once we both finished, Molly and I joined the team for my least favorite activities: wind sprints and agility drills. Coach Kim called this the "cool down." I called it the "pass out." Just to keep my mind off the agony, I played some math games in my head. While everyone else counted from one through 10, I counted in square roots: 1, 4, 9, 16, 25, 36, 49, 64, 81, 100.

"What are you doing?" Anita asked as she overheard my quiet counts.

I hesitated, not sure whether I should tell her the truth. "Nothin'."

"You're counting in square roots, aren't you?" asked another teammate, Samantha Smith.

The City's Brightest Stars academic competition was three weeks away, and I had to be ready.

"Maybe," I said.

Samantha laughed at me, but I didn't care. I liked being smart.

"You're in that genius competition, aren't you?" Anita asked.

"It's not a genius competition," I said defensively.

Coach Kim blew the whistle, and I started to jump rope.

"You're really smart, aren't you?" Samantha asked as she waited her turn.

With my cardiovascular system on overload, I had no desire to speak, so I ignored the question. I fought through every second of pain and survived the entire ten minutes of torture. *All right, I admit it. I'm not a great practice player. I'm more of a gamer.* I performed like a champion with the heat up, the crowd roaring, and my team's reputation on the line. *Now if my coach would only put the gamer in the game!*

"Be ready tomorrow," Coach Kim called out at the end of practice. "I'm going to try and wear the other team down by playing everyone."

I rolled my eyes at her rotten, low-down lie, knowing I would have to see it to believe it. Coach Kim had made the same promise eight times before, and not once did I receive equal playing time with everyone else. So much for the glory days of being an eighth grader. Even most of the seventh graders played more than I did. Three of the eighth graders who hardly played at all last year were getting more time than me. I averaged 10.4 minutes of playing time per match. They averaged 12.6.

I wasn't about to throw in the towel. Like a true champion, I stayed after practice and hit a few balls over the net. I knew I could hit a mean, powerful serve and I loved it. Coach Kim turned to watch me. The butterflies fluttered in my stomach as I smacked the ball as hard as I could. It barely made it to the net.

"That ball is lopsided," I called out. "We need some new ones."

I peeked at Coach Kim out of the corner of my eye, hoping she would give me another chance. As she turned away and went to her office, I clutched my wrist in pain.

"Are you all right?" Penny asked.

"I think I have tendonitis," I insisted. "Or maybe I tore something."

"Hang in there, Wil," Penny assured me.

I stared hopelessly at the ground.

After a few minutes we all retreated to the locker room. I opened my locker and a pile of books fell on the floor. I picked them up and tried to stuff all of them into my bag.

"Give me some of those," Penny said, who as usual

was always looking out for her friends. "You're going to break your back trying to carry all these books down Broadway."

Anita's mom picked us all up in a van and dropped Molly, Penny, and me off at the corner of Broadway and Woodside, which happened to be the home of our favorite hangout, Anderson Park.

"Let's play a game before we go home," Molly suggested, running toward the courts. Penny jogged alongside of her.

"I can't!" I called out. "I've got to study."

"One game," Molly said, waving me over.

"Come on! You need a stress break," Penny added.

I took a deep breath and threw my heavy bag over my shoulder. Forget the yoga, massages, and bubble baths I'd spoil myself with later in life when I had law and business degrees. For now, with my tight budget, the best way to get relief as a Ballplayer was to just go down to the park and beat myself up in a game of basketball.

"Hey!" I called out. "Wait up!"

Just as Molly and Penny both whipped around, three books slipped from my arms and fell to the ground. I sighed as my friends jogged over to me, and each took two books to lighten my load.

"If we're dragging your books around the park like this," Molly said, "you'd better win that competition."

A threat was sometimes Molly's strange way of showing that she cared.

"Thanks for the pep talk, Mo," I added.

She ignored my wisecrack as we hustled over the sandlot and met the boys on the courts.

"We've got next!" Molly called out as she and Penny dumped all of my books into a pile.

"Excuse me, Mo," I said. "Are you going to pay for those damages?"

"Sorry," Molly replied, neatly stacking the books.

"Are you here to study or play ball?" said Jeffrey "J.J." Jasper, who was a regular at Anderson Park.

Eddie Thompson looked at us and scoffed. "This is a park, not a library," he said.

"You wouldn't know what a library is," Molly shot back.

"Okay, creampuff," Eddie replied.

Now right there was some bona fide you-stink, you'll-be-wishing-you-hadn't-said-that trash talk. Eddie, who happened to be the biggest bully on Broadway Avenue, also led the neighborhood in the trash talk department. Of course, Molly O'Malley was a close second.

"I don't know, *ladies*," Eddie continued, knowing how much we couldn't stand his tone when he called us ladies. "You're probably tired from volleyball practice. You don't want to play against us today."

"Give it up, Eddie," Penny said.

"We're ready!" Molly shouted. "Let's go!"

"There are five of us and three of you," Eddie pointed out.

"So?" Molly shot back.

I glanced over my shoulder and saw Angel Russomano and Rosie Jones jog over toward us.

"We've got five," Penny announced. "All the Ballplayers are here."

My four friends and I had earned our nickname after

9

playing in a summer basketball league. Being called a Ballplayer sent shivers up my spine, as if we were a rock band or a traveling show. We were five girls on our way to becoming legend in the city. The Broadway Ballplayers. A living legend.

We hustled Rosie and Angel into the game and checked the ball. I guarded Eddie because I was the only one who could physically match up to him. He tried his best, but he couldn't push me around. I rebounded like a champion. After every one of my phenomenal plays, I reminded myself that I was clearly one of the all-time greatest rebounders who had ever played at Anderson Park. I had to let my friends in on the fun, so I left the scoring up to Penny (10 points), the steals up to Ro (five thefts), the sweet passes up to Angel-cake (seven assists), and the diving all over the place to Mo (lost count).

"Next basket is point-game," Penny called out.

We were up 14–13 and all we needed was one more hoop to wrap up the day. A loose ball hit the ground, and four players dived for it. I didn't even consider scraping my tired body against the asphalt. That was Molly's department.

"Get it, Mo!" I cheered.

Molly wound up at the bottom of the pile with her arms, hands, and legs wrapped around the ball.

"Agh!" someone screamed.

All the players stood up except Eddie. He looked down at his right knee and held his breath. Then he shrieked as he watched the blood ooze from a cut on his knee and run down his leg. He started yelping and crying worse than any kid I'd ever seen in my entire life. I waited for him to crack into a smile and say he was just playing with us, but this was no joke.

"Mommy!" he screamed. "Mommy! Mommy!"

His words stung me, but I didn't say anything. I looked at Molly and her eyes were wide with surprise. The sight of blood had totally freaked Eddie out.

"Relax!" Molly said. "You're fine. It's just a little blood."

"Mommy! Mommy!" Eddie whined.

I shook my head in disbelief. We all knew Eddie couldn't stand his mother. He talked about how she was never home and left him to take care of his little sister alone. But he kept calling her name. I walked over and looked down at him.

"There's so much blood!" he squealed.

"Control the bleeding by applying pressure," I told him.

"But it hurts!" he yelled.

I rolled my eyes and added, "Use a clean dressing or covering to avoid infection."

Eddie took a deep breath, looked up at me, and asked, "How do you know all of this?"

"I do my health homework."

"We don't have anything clean," J.J. said. "We're all sweaty."

I looked to the side of the court and noticed J.J.'s long-sleeved T-shirt. I turned to him and asked, "You don't really want that ratty old shirt, do you?"

"Oh, man, come on. It's my favorite ratty old T-shirt."

"But it's been washed, right?" I said.

"Yeah," J.J. said reluctantly.

"You say you're his friend?" I prodded.

J.J. sighed and then jogged over to pick up his shirt. He came back and handed it to me, and I wrapped it around the cut.

"Hold it there for a few minutes," I said.

"Do you know what you're doing?" Eddie asked.

"What's the matter, Eddie?" Molly asked. "You can't handle a girl taking care of you?"

"Cut him some slack, Mo," Penny said, and Molly backed off.

I picked up Eddie's leg and elevated it.

"What are you doing?" he yelled.

"Elevating the cut above your heart," I explained.

"Do we really have to be doing all of this?" Eddie said as his eyes shifted around the crowd.

"I think you might need stitches," I said as I got a closer look.

"Oh, no!" Eddie shrieked. "It hurts! It hurts! Mommy! Mommy!"

Stop saying that! I shook my head and dropped his leg.

"Ahh!" Eddie screamed again.

"What a wimp," Molly muttered. "Are we going to finish the game or what?"

"Can't you see this guy is still hysterical?" J.J. said. "It's over for today."

"Come on, J.," Penny pleaded. "He's all right. We can finish."

Eddie kept moaning.

"Should we call the paramedics?" Rosie joked quietly.

We all laughed out loud, which made Eddie's white face turn red with anger. The good part was that he finally stopped crying. He finally stopped saying, "Mommy! Mommy! Mommy!"

I didn't like it when he said that, because I didn't have a mother.

Chapter 2

After the game we walked down Broadway Avenue, said our goodbyes, and went our separate ways. I sometimes wished that the Ballplayers all lived together in one big dormitory like the Olympic teams. Instead of houses, we would have living quarters with the same number of rooms, the same kind of car, and the same budget. I wished for all these things because I didn't have a house like the rest of my friends, and I was at least a few years away from making my first million.

It was not as if any of the kids on Broadway had a lot of money or fancy cars. I just knew that my family had less than most folks. We lived in the Uptown Apartments, where people moved in and out of our building so much that I made the 100-day rule. I did not

14

become close friends with anyone in our building until I had seen them for at least 100 days. Unless a person or family passed the 100-day rule, I stuck to my policy of only making friends with the kids and people in the houses on Broadway. My friendships were the safest with them.

I pulled open the front door of my building and headed right for the stairs. I didn't even try to take the elevator because it hardly ever worked. I climbed up sixty-four steps and felt my thighs burn with every lunge. To help pass the time and pain, I started calling out the names of all the U.S. presidents in chronological order.

"George Washington, John Adams, Thomas Jefferson, James Madison . . ." I smiled when I added a new name at the end: Wilma Rudolph Thomas.

I took out my key, unlocked our apartment door, and looked at the usual scene. Clothes, toys, and dishes were scattered all over the living room. My six-year-old sister Louise came around the corner and said, "Hey, hey! What do you say?"

"I say gimme five, Lou-Lou!" I stuck out my hand, and she ran up to me and wound up. I pulled my hand away and she missed. She giggled and then tried again. She still missed. She grabbed my hand and held it still while she slapped it.

"Gotcha!" she said proudly.

I looked around the apartment and waited for the rest of the troops to emerge from their hiding spots and favorite corners of our tiny apartment. Johnny, Blake, and Ricki, who were my wild stepbrothers, moved into the living room like a pack of bees. They started running in their little circles, giggling, chatting, then screaming and yelling. My head began to pound.

"How come you're late?" I heard a voice call out.

I turned. It was my father's wife, Vicki. Legally Vicki was my stepmother, since they had been married for about a year, but I didn't really dig referring to her by a word that contained *mother*.

Vicki walked into the living room with a full plate of food.

"I stopped to play ball at the park," I explained.

"I was just a little worried, that's all," she said.

Worried? I didn't think Vicki ever worried about me.

"There's some leftover chicken on the stove," she said.

Vicki never had time to clean, but she always had plenty of time to cook for herself and the boys. I dropped my bag down and walked through a pile of shoes to get to the kitchen. Louise skipped along behind me and I smiled. Then I noticed the mess in the sink and on the table and I groaned.

"I'll help," Louise offered.

"No," I said. "I'll do it."

I went back into the living room and pulled a notebook out of my bag. I opened it up to a page and set it next to the sink. With the chicken reheating in the oven and my hands scrubbing dishes in the sink, I read my vocabulary words and made up sentences using them in my mind.

*The **oblivious** Vicki has no concept of how embarrassing it is to **subsist** in such an **unruly** apartment.*

Sideline Blues by Wil

*I sometimes live **vicariously** through my friend Penny, who is a sports **phenomenon**. My **pugnacious** friend Molly is always ready to fight.*

"What are you doing?" Louise asked as I finished cleaning.

"Studying." I sat down at the table with a plate of hot chicken and my notebook.

"When is that contest?" she asked.

"Soon."

"Can I go?" she asked.

"Maybe," I said.

"I really want to go," she stated boldly.

Even though Louise was only six, she and I both understood the slim chance of our father showing up to take her. Instead of guessing whether or not my father even remembered my being in the Brightest Stars competition, I thought positively and dreamed big. I imagined him showing up, dressed in a suit and tie and looking proud. I would see him from across the room, break down, and start to cry. So would everyone else around me. With the tears still fresh in my eyes, I would answer every question correctly and go on to win the world championship. It would be so beautiful.

"Can we read a book?" Louise asked.

"Sure," I said. "Let's go in my room."

After reading two books, I tucked Louise into bed. Then I studied straight through to midnight. As a cooldown, I glanced over all the words that began with the letter *q*. Then I read the *W* section of an old encyclopedia the school had let me borrow.

I stayed up until 12:15 A.M. in hopes of hearing my father come home from his late shift. As time passed, my mind raced in fear. *What if he hurt himself at the plant? It's so loud with all the machines, no one would be able to hear him. Maybe I should call to see if he's okay.* I went out to the kitchen, picked up the phone, hung it up immediately, and marched back into my room. I figured that he must have gone out with his friends after work. Then I considered the possibility of one of his drinking buddies driving my father home. *What if something happened to him?*

I woke up early in the morning and anxiously rolled over. I noticed a red cup sitting on my nightstand and breathed a sigh of relief. *Yes! Thank you!* My father always left me a cup of orange juice just in case I got thirsty during the night, which was something he started doing after my mother couldn't anymore. Seeing the cup meant that he had made it home safely.

I wrapped my hands around the cup and gulped down every drop. I licked my lips, said, "Ahhhh!" and grinned at an imaginary television camera.

When all the juice was gone, I stepped out of bed only to be zapped with pain. A heavy throb pulsed in my knee. I grabbed my chair and limped to my desk. I opened my human anatomy book and searched for the exact spot in my knee where I felt the pain.

"Must be the anterior cruciate ligament," I muttered. "Or maybe it's a stress fracture in the patellar or a second-degree sprain of the posterior cruciate."

As the pain slowly faded, I wondered how Eddie was holding up after the life-threatening scratch on his knee.

I doubted that Eddie's mother had taken the time to take a look at his cut.

"Good morning," my father mumbled as he walked past my bedroom door.

"Hi," I said with a smile. Limping out to the hallway, I followed my father into his bedroom. "I have a game today."

"Basketball?" my dad asked as he sat down on the bed.

"No, volleyball," I told him. "Basketball season hasn't started yet."

"Oh," my dad said. "That's right."

I waited for my father to say that he might come and watch me play. I waited for a few more seconds, but he said nothing.

"It's at three-thirty," I added. "At Washington School."

"Maybe I'll stop by," he said. "I'll see."

I grinned at the sound of the word *maybe*. My dad closed his eyes and rested his head on the pillow. Vicki, who was still in bed, had not moved. I pretended not to be bothered by the fact that she didn't even wish me a "good morning." I skipped out of his room and then clutched my aching knee.

"Ow!" I screamed.

The house remained silent. No replies, no concern, nothing. I limped quietly into the kitchen, thinking I could have passed out or had a heart attack in the hallway and no one would have stirred.

Louise walked into the room and sat down quietly at the table. As I ate breakfast, I held up flashcards with letters and numbers for Louise to read. She loved playing games, and I always liked keeping her busy. I didn't want her to stop and think about how tough our life was at home. I didn't want her to think she was missing out on anything.

"You've got to keep moving on in order to leave some things behind," I told her.

"Like what things?" she asked.

"Lots of stuff," I said. "You've got to keep moving on."

She just shook her head at me as if I were speaking in a different language. I don't know. Maybe I was. Some things about our family didn't make a whole lot of sense to me. Like how devastated my father was after losing my mother. What I didn't understand was how within two years, he began dating again. He never talked about my mother, which made me feel like I shouldn't, either. I assumed it would be easier that way. I was scared to know his true feelings. Sometimes I wondered if he loved Vicki more than he loved my mother, but I never asked.

On the ride to school I sat with Molly, Penny, and Rosie. Molly, who had a reputation for being grumpy before ten A.M., leaned her head against the window and closed her eyes. Rosie was so quiet most of the time, we always joked that we had forgotten what her voice sounded like. Penny, popular and friendly as always, spent a lot of time chatting with a bunch of kids who were all different ages. Angel wasn't on the bus with us because she was in high school. I was the oldest Ballplayer when Angel wasn't around, so I carried a lot of responsibility on my shoulders. I felt I had to set a good example. I cracked open my dictionary and started reading all the words that began with the letter *r*.

"What are you doing?" Eddie interrupted.

I looked up and saw his beady eyes glaring down at me. I closed the dictionary and slid it into my bag.

"You're reading the dictionary, aren't you?" he asked with an annoying laugh.

I felt my blood pressure rise.

"Can you tell me how to spell something?" he asked. "Can you spell *dork*? Or how about *geek*? What about *S-Q-U-A-R-E*? What does that spell?"

I shook my head, glared at him, and said, "I'm impressed, Eddie. I didn't think you knew how to spell *square*. Keep working hard and maybe you'll pass spelling this year."

"Shut up, you four-eyed fat girl!" he said defensively.

Suddenly all my strength melted. I appreciated my glasses because I could hardly see without them. But I hated being called fat. I was not fat. Even if I was a little healthier than others, it was nobody else's business but my own. *I can't stand you, Eddie!* I thought as I stuck my nose in the air and pulled my jacket over my body.

"Leave her alone, Eddie!" Molly warned.

"Okay, Porky," Eddie scoffed.

A bunch of boys in the back started laughing.

"You're so stupid, Eddie," Molly said. "Remember yesterday at the park? How's your scrape, Eddie? Do you remember calling for your mommy? And how Wil helped you? Or did your empty head forget already?"

A few other people started to laugh, but at Eddie this

time. I grinned, loving every second of seeing Eddie put in his place.

"Let it go, Mo," Penny said. "You keep talking like that, and you'll be no better than Eddie."

Molly sank down in her seat. "He shouldn't be so mean to people," she grumbled. "It's not right."

Penny sat down next to me and said quietly, "Don't pay any attention to him."

"I don't even know why I helped him in the first place," I said. "I'm not taking any more time out of my day for that sorry kid."

I spent the rest of the ride staring out the window while I silently practiced counting to fifty in French, Italian, Spanish, German, and Japanese. When I hesitated on one number, I frantically pulled my book out of my bag and read my study sheet.

"Relax," Penny said. "You're making me nervous."

"I just want to make sure. I've got to be prepared."

"You are," Molly said. "You've never gotten a B in your entire life. You are Miss Prepared."

"I wouldn't mess with you," Rosie agreed.

"I don't want this to be the first time I mess up," I said.

"Don't sweat it, Wil," Penny said. "You'll be able to teach the judges a thing or two."

I kept flipping through my pages as we walked through school. I *had* to win the competition. The whole school was counting on me to bring home the victory. If I didn't win, I would punish myself by not letting myself play at the park ever again.

We walked to our lockers. The bell rang and our principal marched down the hallway, wading through the morning rush. Mobs of kids threw their books inside their lockers and hurried off to class. Molly and Penny jogged off to the seventh-grade wing in the basement; Rosie hustled off to the sixth-grade classes on the second floor; and I took my time walking into my eighth-grade homeroom just across the hall. Having no stairs to climb was one of the luxuries of finally being in eighth grade at Lincoln School.

"See you later," I called out.

I walked into our classroom and smiled at my favorite teacher, Mrs. Ramirez.

"Good morning, Wilma," she said. "How are you today?"

"Très bien!" I said. *"Pourquoi?"*

"You look tired, Wil," she said. "Have you been staying up late studying?"

I nodded. "Where's my partner?" I asked.

"She went to the office," Mrs. Ramirez said. "She'll be right back."

I waited anxiously for my Brightest Stars teammate to arrive. Within seconds, Peaches McCool walked through the doorway.

"Hey, girl," Peaches said to me with a pearly smile. "What's up?"

"I'm nervous," I said. "Aren't you?"

Peaches shook her head and looked at me with her pretty almond-shaped eyes. "We can do it. I know we can. We've studied harder than anybody else in the city."

"Did you go over Ditto 25 Vocab?" I asked.

"You know it. Let's quiz each other."

We grabbed our chairs and began testing each other

just as morning announcements began. Everyone quieted down when they heard Mr. Gordon, our principal, speak over the public address system.

"Please rise for the pledge of allegiance," his voice boomed.

I recited the pledge loudly and clearly, as did everyone else. Mrs. Ramirez and Mr. Gordon let us hear it if we didn't pay our respects to our country and to each other. After the pledge Mr. Gordon began the announcements.

"The seventh- and eighth-grade volleyball team will be playing at Washington School this afternoon at three-thirty. Show some school spirit and cheer on our team!"

"They stink," Eddie muttered from the back of the room.

"You stink," I said.

"One more announcement. Peaches McCool and Wilma Thomas will be representing Lincoln School in the Brightest Stars City-Wide Competition in two weeks. They've been working very hard. Be sure to wish them well."

My nerves tingled. I pushed my glasses up on my nose. I felt my face get hot, and I looked at Peaches. She smiled at everyone who was staring at us. Everybody loved Peaches McCool. She was as sweet and as cool as her first and last name, and she was smart, too. Really smart. Both of us were in the running for valedictorian of our eighth-grade class. We never talked about any rivalry. Instead we both studied like crazy to win the competition for the school. The competition for first and second of the class could wait.

"I'll see you two early tomorrow morning for our study session," Mrs. Ramirez told us. "I'd like you to focus on politics tonight so I can quiz you tomorrow."

I nodded eagerly at our mentor. Mrs. Ramirez had taken Peaches and me under her wing the first day of school and told us about this competition. She felt we could be the first team in the history of Lincoln School to bring home the gold. For almost six weeks she gave us almost four times as much homework as she gave everyone else.

"The only place that success comes before work is in the dictionary," she preached.

We listened to every word she said.

"Why don't you come over to my house on Sunday for dinner?" she asked. "Just so we can study in a different place."

My eyes grew wide in amazement. I had never been over to a teacher's house for dinner.

"Cool," said Peaches. "That will be fun."

"I'm there," I said excitedly.

Then Mrs. Ramirez stopped and looked at me. "Are you sure you're not too tired, Wil?"

"I'm fine," I said as I remembered how I had rushed out of the house to make the bus. I looked down at my wrinkled clothes and ran my hand over my tangled braids.

"Maybe you should take some time off from all the sports you're playing," Mrs. Ramirez said. "I want you to make sure you get plenty of rest."

"I'll be fine," I said. "I hurt my knee in practice yesterday, but I'll be all right. It hurt pretty bad this morning, so I'll stop by and see Nurse Carol before practice."

I rubbed my knee and looked into the eyes of my teacher.

"Are you sure you're all right?" she asked me with concern.

"I'll be all right," I said. "I have a high tolerance for pain."

"Are you going to be able to play?" Peaches asked.

I thought about Coach Kim and convinced myself that she would see the light and give a true ballplayer a chance.

"I think I'm starting today," I told my teacher and my classmate.

"Really?" Mrs. Ramirez said.

"Yep," I said proudly. "It's a big game for us. I can't let my teammates down. They're counting on me."

Chapter 3

"Nurse Carol," I called out after I gently knocked on her door. "May I come in?"

Our school nurse didn't even look up from her desk. "Yes, Wil," she called out.

As I walked closer to Nurse Carol, she removed her reading glasses and looked up at me.

"What can I do for you today?" she asked with a smile.

"I woke up this morning and my knee hurt really bad," I said. I bent over and clutched my sore knee. "Right here."

Nurse Carol looked down at my leg. I had changed into my volleyball uniform so she could perform a full examination.

"It doesn't look swollen."

"It hurts," I insisted. "What about my game today?"

"Does it hurt too much to play?" she asked.

"I've *got* to play," I pleaded. "It's a big game. We're talking *huge.*"

"Huge?" Nurse Carol said with a smile.

"Yes," I insisted. "Coach Kim might start me. She said she's going to play everyone. I've never started this season. So I figure today is my day. I can't miss my chance."

"Let's see if that knee is all right then," Nurse Carol said. "Have a seat on the table."

I limped across the room and hopped up on the table. Nurse Carol's strong hands grabbed my leg and moved it around.

"Do you think it's my posterior cruciate ligament or my anterior cruciate?" I asked.

"Neither," she said as she shook her head at me. Then she grinned. I know sometimes my memory amazed people, but now was not the time to be cracking smiles.

"What is it, then?" I begged.

"A sore knee," she said. "Or growing pains."

"That's it?" I gasped. "Are you sure?"

"Would you like a second opinion?" she asked.

I shook my head. I trusted Nurse Carol with every sniffle, cough, ache, and pain in my body. She reached in the freezer and pulled out a pack of ice.

"Ice it before and after the game," she said.

"How long?" I asked.

"About twenty minutes each time," she said. "You should tell Coach Kim that you might not be 100 percent."

"I can't!" I said. "I have to be able to play!"

"Just be careful," she said.

"Is that your final prescription?" I asked. "Ice and be careful?"

"Stretch out your legs before the game," she said. "And if it really hurts, then come out of the game."

I lifted my head and smiled confidently. "You should really be a doctor."

Nurse Carol smiled as she returned to her seat. "Why don't *you* go to school to be a doctor so someday you can take care of *me*?"

"Dr. Thomas," I said reverently. "I kind of like the way that sounds."

Nurse Carol laughed. "Good luck in your game today, Wil. I'll try to stop by."

"Thanks," I said excitedly.

My knee felt better the second I walked out of the room. I clutched my ice pack and jogged toward the locker room and met up with my teammates. We grabbed our gym bags, ran out the back door, and climbed into a van for the short drive to Washington School.

"What's with the ice pack?" Samantha asked me. "Are you hurt?"

"Nurse Carol thinks it's okay," I whispered. "I just don't want to tear a ligament or make it worse."

"You might tear a ligament?" Anita asked.

"Don't worry. I have a high tolerance for pain."

Molly and Penny asked me what was wrong.

"No need to fear," I assured them. "I'm still playing."

"I didn't want you wimping out on us," Molly said.

"I would never do such a thing," I said.

Molly looked at me and rolled her eyes.

"What?" I said defensively.

"Nothin'," Molly replied.

But I knew what she was thinking. During the previous season, Molly had counted how many times I bent over to tie my shoes during our running drills at basketball practice.

"Twenty-eight times this year," she informed me at our last practice. "And half the time you bent over, you were untying your shoes just so you had a reason to tie them."

Maybe sometimes I did take things a little too far.

"Are you going to tape up your knee or wear a brace?" Penny asked.

It sounded like a good idea. A little preventive medicine couldn't hurt.

"I've got an extra knee sleeve if you want to borrow it," she added.

Penny pulled out a blue knee brace, and I accepted it with a thank-you. I finished icing my knee and slid on the brace. "It feels better already."

As we walked into the gym, all the ice made me think about water. Within seconds I *really* had to use the rest room.

"Where's the rest room?" I asked.

"Two doors down on your left," Molly called out surely.

I jogged down the hallway and stopped in front of the second door. I didn't notice a GIRLS or BOYS sign. But I didn't have too much time to think, so I just pushed the door open. Then I almost passed out. The scary sight of a locker room full of boys standing in their underwear met my eyes. I froze in shock and humiliation as they screamed and danced around to cover up. I bolted back to my friends. My bladder was about to explode.

"Molly!" I yelled.

Molly and Penny whipped around. She looked at me with a straight face and asked, "What's wrong with you?"

"You just sent me into the boys' locker room!" I hollered, and I slugged her on the arm.

Molly's blue eyes lit up, and she scooped her hand over her mouth. Penny burst out laughing.

"I just made up where the bathroom was," Molly explained. "I didn't think you'd actually listen to me!"

"Normal people don't joke about things like that," I said. Then I could feel everyone within earshot staring at me. "I'm *so* embarrassed."

"Were they naked?" Anita asked with a grin.

"No!" I said. "They were in their underwear."

The whole team laughed hysterically.

After a few more minutes of giggling and teasing, Coach Kim interrupted us. "Settle down and let's warm up. We've got a game to play."

I asked Coach Kim directions to the real rest room, then I hurried down the hall. I slowly opened the door and peeked inside. No boys. I hustled in, used the facilities, flew out the door, and ran down the hall back to the gym. I never wanted to see those boys ever again.

Of course, during warm-ups, the whole boys' team emerged from the locker room. As my teammates chuckled, I didn't look at anyone except Coach Kim, who was smacking hits right at me. I tried to slide under one, but it ricocheted off my shoulder. I whacked the next ball so hard that it hit the ceiling. Finally, after a few seconds, the boys left the gym and I relaxed. I made one last bump and felt a rush of confidence. I couldn't wait for Coach Kim to call out the starting lineup. The ref blew the whistle, and I hustled into the huddle and screamed our team cheer.

"Spike 'em, beat 'em, make 'em eat it, dig it, yeah!"

Coach Kim looked down at her clipboard.

"Molly, Penny, Samantha, Jozette, Amy, and Anita," she said. "Hustle on out there!"

I was so crushed, so entirely devastated, that I didn't just sit down. I collapsed onto the bench so hard that my back throbbed in pain.

"But you've promised us eight times this year that you're going to play everyone," I mumbled to our coach.

Coach Kim looked at me and her eyes narrowed. "No *buts!*"

I cupped my hand over my motor mouth and mumbled, "Sorry. I know you don't like us complaining. But— whoops. There's your favorite word again." I laughed nervously, cleared my throat, and then asked, "I just still would really like to know why you keep breaking your promise."

"Let me do the coaching and you do the playing," she said.

"But you don't play me!" I shot back.

"Don't be so selfish," she said. "This is a team game."

I muttered, "Whatever."

Sideline Blues by Wil

Coach Kim's icy glare grabbed hold of me. I decided at that moment to take the Fifth Amendment of the Constitution and keep quiet before I incriminated myself any further. I sank down in my seat and ended the conversation. Another word, especially one that began with the letter *b*, and Coach Kim would send me clear off the bench and out of the gym.

As the game started, I pulled myself together. I rooted for my friends even though I desperately wanted a chance to be out on the court. Every time Coach Kim glanced at the bench, I cheered like a raving fool. But the only substitution she made was Karly for Jozette. That was it. Like a true champion, I kept howling and clapping, but Coach Kim couldn't have cared less. We trounced Washington 15–3 in the first game, and I didn't see one minute of action.

As our team took the floor for the second game, I thought about sitting silent in protest. Then Penny glanced over at the bench and said, "Come on, Wil! Get us going!"

I folded my arms across my chest and turned away.

"Please?" Penny asked.

I huffed, jumped up, and started hooting and hollering.

"Serve it up, P.!"

"Cover the net, Mo and Jo!"

Soon all the girls on the floor were clapping and cheering. Two points into the game, Coach Kim called out my name.

"Wil," she said. "Go in for Samantha."

I jumped up from my spot and said, "Yes, baby! Yes!"

All my bench buddies called out "Sub!" to the referee, and I strutted to the edge of the court and waited. The ref, standing on her perch above the net, waved me on the floor. I slapped hands with Sam and jogged to my position.

"Let's go, now!" I shouted. "Be aggressive!"

Molly served the ball over the net and the volley began. I danced around, positioning myself for every possible hit in every possible direction. A few more passes and bumps were made. Then *BOOM!* The middle hitter nailed the ball almost right down my throat. She hit it so fast that I didn't even have time to react. As the other team roared in celebration, I looked over at Coach Kim and she gritted her teeth. I looked nervously around at my teammates, but they supported me. "Shake it off, Wil. You'll get the next one."

I rolled my eyes and rested my hand on my hip. I didn't *want* another one like that. An Olympic athlete couldn't have hit the spike that almost took my head off. It must have been going eighty miles an hour. I wanted somebody—anybody—to tell me that it wasn't my fault. *Nobody could have hit that ball!*

Three plays later the same girl crushed me with almost the same exact hit. Except this one seemed like it was traveling at approximately ninety-five miles an hour. I looked at my front row, desperate for some help.

"Can I get a blocker?" I asked.

The whistle blew and I turned toward the referee. I spotted Samantha standing next to Coach Kim, and they were both looking at me. I turned over my shoulder, hoping to see someone standing behind me. "Who, me?" I asked.

My coach nodded and motioned for me to come over.

"But, Coach Kim—"

She glared at me and gritted her teeth. "Wilma," she warned.

I shook my head and jogged off the court in total humiliation. I wanted to run right out of the gym. I looked over to some of the regulars on the bench, and their wide, concerned eyes told me to hang in there. This was all part of being a scrub. I decided that I couldn't jump ship. I moped over to my seat and joined the scrub club.

"I've got the blues," I said to my bench-warming buddies.

"Uh-huh," one teammate said.

I turned my words into a little song and continued. "Oh, I've got the sideline blues. The back-achin', frustratin' sideline blues."

"I hear you," another added.

They all nodded. I kept humming as I pondered the thought of being stuck on the bench for eternity, but luckily Coach Kim subbed me in three plays later. When she called out my name, I considered a boycott. But a teammate pushed me and said, "Hurry up!"

Thirty seconds into the game Anita jumped in front of me for a bump that clearly should have been mine. We collided and both went crashing to the ground. I felt my ankle twist the wrong way. The pain made me cringe. I glared at Anita and snapped, "That was mine!"

"Sorry," she said softly.

I stood up, limped around in a small spot, and took deep breaths. Then the whistle blew. I didn't even have to look this time. I had already felt Coach Kim's eyes on me. I dragged myself off the floor and returned to my spot on the bench. I looked around the gym hoping to see my father, but he wasn't there. I wondered if he was sleeping. Or if he just plain forgot all about me. Then I searched the gym for Nurse Carol. She wasn't there, either. I needed her. *What if I reinjured my knee? What about my ankle? This could be serious!*

Our team went on a run, and we won the second game, clinching the match. The coaches decided to play a third game "for fun." This third game was for players like me—players ill with the sideline blues. Playing was supposed to make me happy, but I wasn't. My knee, ankle, and feelings hurt, not to mention my back and bottom from falling down on the bench.

"Are you okay to play?" Coach Kim asked.

"I'm fine," I answered. "Couldn't be better." She looked at me, trying to decide if I was being sarcastic. "I'm ready if you need me, Coach," I added with a smile.

I played with a mix of starters and bench warmers. Not to brag—but I was awesome—I didn't make a single mistake. I even spiked the ball twice. After I scored two consecutive points, I looked over at Coach Kim and shook my head. *How come I'm not starting?*

The game ended and I didn't say a word. When we got on the bus, I flipped open a book and started reading. As I read the information, my confidence barometer slowly grew from negative numbers into positive ones.

Sideline Blues by Wil

Even though I felt like a fool on the bench, I smiled proudly with all my friends as I read my favorite books. My mind was my power plant. I could see our names in pink, neon, and yellow lights.

WILMA RUDOLPH THOMAS AND PEACHES MCCOOL
BRIGHTEST STARS CHAMPS OF THE UNIVERSE

Later as we walked down Broadway Avenue, J.J. and Eddie crossed our path.

"Did you win?" J.J. asked.

"Yeah," Molly said. "Where were you?"

"We had some business to take care of," Eddie said.

"Yeah, right," Penny countered. "Where's your school spirit?"

"How many spikes did you have, P.?" J.J. asked.

Penny shrugged. "Mo had more than me," she said.

"Yeah, right, P.," Molly replied. "If you add up every one I got in the last month."

Everyone kept talking as if I wasn't even there. Nobody asked how I did. Nobody asked if I played. I waited for Eddie to make a comment about having to take splinters out of my bottom from sitting on the pine, but he didn't. I was glad.

We all headed home for dinner. I walked slowly up the stairs. I didn't count in any foreign language. I didn't call out the Presidents. I walked slowly up the stairs and sang a song.

> *I got the blues.*
> *Oh, I got the blues.*

The Broadway Ballplayers

The back-achin', frustratin',
Sideline Blues.
No news, no news.
All I got today is
The Sideline Blues.

The melody of my beautiful voice echoed through the stairwell. When I opened the door of our apartment, my little sister greeted me. "Hey, hey! Did you win?"

I nodded. "What did I tell you about saying 'hey' so much?" I said. "People don't like being called 'Hey.' "

"I know," Louise said. "Daddy already told me."

I was glad to hear that my father had taken time to pass on an important message to Lou-Lou. Maybe he had even noticed that she had developed some weird habits and sayings. One day she had insisted that her name was KiKi. We had no idea why she had chosen that particular name.

"Just call me KiKi," she said.

She wouldn't answer to anything else, so we called her KiKi for a week. Then she announced that she had changed her name back to Louise. Two weeks later she changed it to Tallulah and then Bobbi. This all happened around the time that my father remarried.

My father walked into the living room that night and said hello. I walked right past him still wearing my uniform and purple knee pads, still upset.

"Where were you this afternoon, Dad?" I asked.

"Here," he said.

"I had a game," I said. "You said you'd come."

"I had to sleep," he said softly as he looked away. "I've got another double shift tonight."

I didn't say anything else. As I prepared dinner, I wondered how many years my father would need to work to pay off all my mother's hospital bills. Three years had already passed. *How many more games will he miss?*

My father left the room and I sang the song of the day.

No news, no news.
All I got today is
The Sideline Blues.

Chapter 4

I woke up in the middle of the night drenched with a cold sweat after having a bad dream. A horrible dream. It was about the Brightest Stars Competition. Five minutes before our starting time, I had to use the rest room. I rushed down the hallway, stopped in front of the door, and made sure that the sign said GIRLS. I checked every letter and took a deep breath. When I pushed open the door, I almost passed out. All the judges were inside, standing in their underwear. I ran down the hallway screaming, "This isn't fair! This isn't fair!" All the other teams laughed at me. I started sobbing. When the judges came out of the rest room and announced that Wil Thomas was disqualified because she couldn't read the sign on the bathroom door, I collapsed. Molly, Penny, Angel, and Rosie dragged me out of the building.

• • •

I had never been so happy to wake up as I was that morning. I took a few breaths and told myself to get a grip. Then I sat at my desk and started studying.

Three hours later Lou-Lou knocked on my door.

"Let's go, slowpoke," she said.

"I'm coming, I'm coming!" I slammed my grammar book shut and dragged myself up from my bed. I wiped the wrinkles out of my bedspread and neatly placed the book back on the shelf of my personal library.

"Come on," Louise whined. "Hurry up!"

"Who said you could give orders?" I asked.

She put her hand on her hip and rolled her eyes.

"You'd better watch yourself, Miss Attitude," I said, and my little sister straightened up.

"I want to play basketball today," she said.

"Um, Lou. Isn't there a little problem?"

"What?" She turned around and looked at me.

"Are you strong enough to hit the rim?" I asked.

"Yes!" she shot back defensively.

She was dreaming, of course.

"I don't know, Lou," I said doubtfully.

She turned and flexed her wiry arms. "Look at how strong I am!"

I shook my head. "You call those muscles?" I rolled up my sleeve to reveal my rock-solid biceps. "Call me The Rock," I said proudly, but Louise ignored me and walked out the door. I hurried to catch up with her. We both raced down the stairs and beat our feet down Broadway Avenue. Just before we turned down Woodside to the park, I told my sister that we had to go pick up Penny and Molly first.

"Why?" she said. "They're big enough to walk down themselves."

"We're the Ballplayers," I said. "Our team is a team for life. We have to stick together."

Just before I called out a team cheer, I noticed Molly's mom raking leaves on the front lawn. Mrs. O'Malley whisked the leaves off the green grass so fast that it looked as if she were vacuuming. Then she bent over, pushed the leaves onto the rake, and flipped it into the wheelbarrow. Her son Kevin wiped his forehead and stood at her side watching in amazement. She ordered him back to work, and he did as he was told without saying a word.

At that moment I remembered how fast my mother could move before she got sick. I remembered the rock-solid muscles in her arms and calves. One day when I was playing in the basement, a pipe fell down and pinned a boy to the floor. Five teenage kids tried to pull the pipe off the poor kid, but it wouldn't budge. I ran up all sixty-four steps and told my mom what had happened. She sprinted down to the basement and swiftly lifted the pipe off the boy, who walked home uninjured. Then she ordered all the kids out of the dangerous basement, ran back upstairs, and finished making dinner. After she left, I walked upstairs with a wide grin and told every kid, "Yeah. Yeah. That's *my* mama."

Molly pushed open her front door, picked up her basketball, tucked it under her arm, and ran up to us.

"Hurry up before my mom makes me start raking again!" she said.

We all looked nervously over our shoulders. Mrs. O'Malley kept working without missing one stroke. I felt a little guilty as we jogged down the street and toward Angel Russomano's house. We ran up the sidewalk and I rang the bell. Angel's father answered.

"Good morning, girls," Mr. Russomano said. He smiled down at us and we greeted him.

"Angel!" he called out. "The Players are here!"

"*Ball*players," Molly politely corrected him. "We're the Ballplayers."

"I'm sorry," he said. He raised his voice with enthusiasm and called out, "The Broadway Ballplayers are here!" Then he looked at us. "How was that?"

"Perfect," I told him.

Molly looked away. She got annoyed when people shortened or messed up our nickname. I couldn't hold anything against Mr. Russomano, especially because he was a minister. I elbowed Molly in the side so she would respectfully respond to the man who was looking right at her.

"We'll let it go just this once," Molly agreed with a sly smile. Mr. Russomano winked at us and disappeared into the house. As we waited for Angel, I looked through the door hoping to see Mrs. Russomano. When I didn't spot her, I had a bad feeling that the rumors were true. Mrs. Russomano must have really left. Angel never talked about it even when we asked. Despite her silence, all of us knew that things weren't good at home. I thought back to the few times I could remember my parents arguing. I could still feel myself get angry inside. I took one long look at Mr. Russomano as he passed by the doorway. *You still have each other. Why can't you just get along?*

Angel and her little brother Gabe came to the door and smiled.

"What's up, Angel-cake?" I asked.

"Not much," she replied.

Both Angel and Gabe came outside and walked over to Rosie's house with us. With her cap flipped backward, a baseball mitt tucked under her arm, and a muffin in her hand, Rosie jogged down the steps. "Anybody want a bite?" she asked.

My mouth watered, but I said no thanks just to be polite like everyone else. Some kids made fun of how much I loved to eat. I didn't care what they said. Every kid in the neighborhood knew that Mrs. Jones could really cook. At my house, good meals were hard to come by with Vicki never in the kitchen and my crazy study schedule. So when somebody worked so hard to cook something, I felt it was disrespectful if I didn't enjoy it. I had a weakness for sweets and Nurse Carol knew it. She told me I should cut back on the doughnuts, cupcakes, and caffeine. For an entire month I wrote down every single thing I ate and gave the list to Nurse Carol. She rewarded me with a basket of fruit.

"Can't I get just one cupcake?" I asked her that day. "I know you have somebody's birthday cupcakes in your little fridge."

Nurse Carol opened the door and removed the last cupcake from the shelf. She took out a knife and cut it in half. I said a toast "To all the people in this world who eat right" and finished the small half of my cupcake. It felt a little strange eating a cupcake in front of my nutritionist. But it wasn't like I never exercised. Big muscles covered my body. I was a healthy girl.

I walked with my friends and grinned as I remembered Mrs. Ramirez's invitation to dinner.

"Mrs. Ramirez is having Peaches and me over for dinner tomorrow night," I told my friends. I was bragging and I knew it. "We're going to study, too."

"You're going to win the competition," Angel said. "You deserve it."

I smiled. "I hope so," I said.

Then last, but certainly not least, we picked up Shantell "Penny" Harris.

"You ready?" Penny said as she skipped down her steps in her matching headband and sweatbands.

Penny's grandmother gave her the nickname Penny so she would have a little luck with her all the time. But my best friend didn't need luck. She had everything: a good head on her shoulders, natural athleticism, a cute smile, and a magnetic personality. At the age of twelve, Penny was already a star on Broadway Avenue.

"Let's roll," she said.

Penny's grandmother stepped out on the porch. She waved and we all called out, "Hi, Grandma!" She smiled and winked at me. Penny's grandmother had helped me out during a tough time in my life. She had lost her husband when she was young and had to raise her children all by herself. I looked down at Lou-Lou and remembered what Penny's grandmother had told me about my sister.

"She needs you," Penny's grandmother had said. "And you need her."

"Can we go now?" Louise asked.

"Yes, Lou," I said. "We're going."

I watched Penny as she coolly dribbled a basketball behind her back and between her legs.

"I heard Beef Potato and Mike are going to be down at the courts today," Penny said. "There should be some good games then."

I sighed. Beef Potato was one of the biggest, best basketball players in town. The poor person stuck with guarding him was almost always yours truly. "Do I have to guard Beef?" I asked, dreading the answer.

"Yes," Molly said. "You don't want us to lose, do you?"

"I'll guard him if you really don't want to," Angel offered.

"No, that's all right, Angel-cake," I said. "I'll sacrifice this beautiful body for the sake of my team. For the sake of my friends. For the sake of the sport of basketball itself."

"Oh, puh-leze quit talking," Penny said with a smile.

As we turned down Woodside, we could see the courts already packed with kids.

"We've got next!" Penny called out. Everyone at the park turned and looked at us. My nerves tingled. I loved hanging out with the Ballplayers.

"There's Beef," Rosie said.

I spotted Beef at the far basket. Nobody really knew Beef's name. Somebody told me it was Tommy Meeks, but he preferred to be called by his nickname at all times.

"Hey, Pork Chop," I said to him as we walked on the courts.

"What's up, Meat Ball?" Penny added.

He grinned. "I only answer to Beef or Potato," he said firmly. "Get it right."

I laughed. Louise came up and tugged on my shirt. "Can I go play on the swings now?" she asked.

"Yeah," I said. "But don't go too far."

She ran off and I shot around with the Ballplayers to get warmed up. I occasionally looked over to check on Louise, and she looked like she was doing just fine by herself.

"Let's get started," J.J. suggested. "How about we pick teams?"

My palms began to sweat. I hated when we picked teams. I looked around at all the good players: Penny, Beef, Cowboy, Molly, Angel, Mike, J.J., Marvin, Rosie . . . My heart began to race. I knew I wasn't going to get picked. I should have just stayed home and exercised my brain.

J.J. and Mike called out to be captains. J.J. made his shot so he picked first, and of course, he picked Penny. The draft went back and forth, and then it came down to the last player for the game. Billy Flanigan and I bit our fingernails and stared at the ground. *Please pick me. I'm good. I'm really good. I can rebound. I can shoot. I can guard Beef!*

Penny whispered something to J.J. He looked at me and called out, "Wil's with us." I smiled as I joined my team, feeling a shot of pride, then guilt, as I left Billy Flanigan all by himself.

47

"You've got next game, Bill," Penny assured him. He nodded sadly as he walked off the court.

I stretched out my body a little bit and then I felt the ache in my knee. I panicked. *I forgot to ice!*

"What's the matter, Wil?" Molly asked as she caught me wincing in pain.

"I forgot to ice my knee today. But don't sweat it. I'll be all right."

For the first five minutes of the game, all I could think about was every possible way I could injure my knee or ankle. But after Beef scored twice in a row, I forgot all about how much my body hurt. I pushed him around and boxed him out. I grabbed one rebound and another. I ran up and down the court like a gazelle. I scored. I cheered. I was The Woman.

"Good job, Wil!" Penny cheered. "Keep it up!"

The next time down the court, I looked at Penny and whispered, "Give me the ball, P." Penny dribbled up the court and bounce-passed the ball to me in the post position. I faked one way, spun around, squared my shoulders up to the hoop, let the shot go, faded away in midair, and kicked my foot out for a little extra style. I let go and the ball fell about three feet short.

"What was that?" Molly asked.

My total and complete airball made me return to planet Earth.

"I'm sorry," I said. "My bad."

"Shake it off, Wil," Penny said.

I tried to bounce back, but all I did was bounce off Beef. He crushed me with all of his post moves. Molly tried to help me out, but Beef just scored on the both of us.

"Could somebody please guard Potato Head?" J.J. called out.

"I am!" I said. "I am!"

Beef carried his team and Penny carried ours. She was everywhere we needed her to be. Penny put all kinds of pressure on the other team and then picked off one of Mike's lazy passes.

"Don't let Beef get the ball," she told us.

Penny's strategy made perfect sense to me. That was my kind of game: Keep the ball away from my player. We won the first game, lost the second, and then ended up winning the last two. Molly turned to me and asked what the scores were for each and every game. I told her all I could remember and asked, "What, do you keep a list?"

"So?" she said defensively. "J.J. keeps track, too."

I shook my head. The only thing I kept track of for the rest of the afternoon were all of my aches and pains, and my little sister.

"Let's go, Lou-Lou!" I called out. "It's time to go."

I searched through the crowd of running and screaming kids. I waited for her to appear, but she didn't.

"Where is Louise?" I asked Penny.

All my friends looked around. Molly shook her head. "Did she go home?" she asked.

"She wouldn't," I said. "Not without me."

Penny called out, "Louise! Has anyone seen Louise?"

All the little kids shrugged. I felt the tears in my eyes. My bottom lip began to quiver. "Where is she?"

Angel patted me on the back and said, "Don't worry, Wil. She's around."

With every second I could feel the pressure build in my chest. I started to think about what I would tell my father. I couldn't go home without my sister. I felt the anger and fear build up inside of me. *Don't do this, Lou!*

"Hey, hey!" a voice called out. "What do you say?"

I looked to my right and saw my smiling sister.

"Where have you been?" I asked firmly.

"I had to go to the bathroom," she said.

I took a deep breath and pulled myself together. "Why didn't you tell me where you were going?"

"I tried telling you," she explained. "But you were playing and I couldn't wait."

"Please don't disappear like that again," I said quietly so my friends couldn't hear.

"Sorry," she said, and then she stared at the ground. "I just had to go."

Louise and I walked home with the Ballplayers. They talked about having a slumber party, but I didn't get excited about the idea like I normally did. All I could think about was studying.

"Why don't you all come over and watch a movie at my house?" Molly asked. "We can hang out in the fort, too."

"I've got to go over to Mrs. Ramirez's tomorrow," I said. "She's going to quiz us."

Everybody else was in except me. I thought about how much I loved hanging out in the small fort Mr. O'Malley had built in the backyard. Then I drew up a list in my mind of all the work I needed to do.

"Two more weeks and this is all over. My life will return to normal," I said.

"No, it won't," Penny said. "Because after you win, you'll be famous."

I smiled. I wondered if I would be able to handle all the attention. *So many people will want to ask me questions. They might ask me to solve world problems and predict their futures.* I decided right then and there that I must have a stance on every issue from gun control to jaywalking. I had to be sharp, witty, profound, and charismatic. I would have to be able to deal with eighth graders all day and world leaders at night. The world leaders I could handle. The eighth graders I wasn't too sure about.

When I arrived home that night, I brought Louise into my room and put a big *X* through that day on my calendar.

"Thirteen days until the competition," I said to her. "Actually, it's twelve days and nine hours."

Louise didn't pay any attention. I shook my head. She was too young to understand why I had to win.

Chapter 5

When Louise crawled into my bed that night, I refused to budge.

"Don't even think about it," I warned her.

My stubborn sister squeezed her small body closer to me.

"Come on, Lou," I groaned.

"Please, can I stay?" She stared at me with sad eyes and curled her bottom lip.

"You're getting too big," I said.

"Please don't make me sleep with them," she begged. Louise had to share a room and a king-size bed with Ricki, Johnny, and Blake. "They snore too much, and Blake still has accidents sometimes."

I huffed and moved over. "No talking or snoring. I have to study."

As Louise grinned and curled under the covers, I started to think about the Brightest Stars Competition and all the preparation I had to do. I needed a lot of work in the politics department. I already knew all the Presidents, but what about the Constitution? *What if they ask me to recite the Preamble? Do I know every word?*

"We the people of the United States, in order to form a more perfect union, establish justice . . ."

"Are you praying?" Louise asked.

"No talking!" I said, but I couldn't deprive her of an answer. "It's the first sentence of the Constitution."

"Oh," she said. "I knew that."

"Shhh!" I continued. *"Insure domestic tranquillity, provide for the common defense . . ."*

"ZZZZzzz . . ." Louise was out like a light. I finished the preamble, reviewed my notes on the Civil War, and closed my eyes. After playing at the park all day, I slept like a baby.

I woke up the next morning and smiled as I took a sip out of the cup of orange juice my father had left on my nightstand. Then I carefully moved Louise's legs out of my way and quietly slid out of bed. I turned on the light over my desk and cracked open my history textbook. As a warm-up, I named all the Presidents and stated every President's political party. In sixth grade I wanted to be a Democrat and in seventh I changed my mind to Republican. Then as a mature, intelligent, worldly eighth grader, I decided to call myself an Independent. If anybody asked what party I belonged to, I would simply state, "Wil's American People Party." W.A.P.P. for short.

The W.A.P.P. would do the following: We would fight relentlessly for equal rights for women. We would find a way for all children to go to college so every person would have a fair chance in our world. We would double the number of doctors to research cancer. We would severely punish children who made fun of other children for being slightly overweight or smart. We would form numerous professional sports leagues. The President (yours truly, of course) would be allowed to play as much as she wanted on any team she chose. And last, W.A.P.P. would fight again for more equal rights for women even on the days they didn't feel like they had any more fight left in them.

"Read me a story," Louise moaned from the bed.

"I'm studying."

"Tell me about what you're studying." She rolled over and looked at me.

"I have a lot of work to do today," I said. "I'm meeting with Mrs. Ramirez and Peaches tonight to study for the competition."

"What's Peaches's real name?" Louise asked.

"Veronica," I replied. "But she prefers to be called Peaches."

"And what's her last name?"

"McCool," I said. "Peaches McCool."

"I wish I had a cool name like yours," Louise said. She sat up in my bed and scratched her chin, staring pensively at the ceiling. I looked at her and wondered what was running through that wild head of hers.

"I've changed my name," she stated boldly.

"What is it this time?" I asked, dreading the answer.

"Banana Anna."

"That's not cool," I said. "It's dumb."

"Banana Anna Thomas is my name," she said. "I won't answer to anything else."

I shook my head at my stubborn sister. "If you have a new name, then I want one too."

I scratched my chin as I stared up at the ceiling, imitating my sister. There was nothing wrong with Wilma Rudolph Thomas except that I couldn't really run like the speed demon. At first I was just playing along with my sister. Then I started thinking that maybe it *was* time for a change. A new name for the competition would give me a new persona. I needed something intimidating. Forceful. Serious. Intelligent. Unique. I picked up my women's history book and flipped through it, stopping at former slave and women's rights leader Sojourner Truth. I read her brief biography, which described how she did as much work in the fields as any man. It also described how she didn't have a chance to go to school, but that didn't stop her from taking a stance on women's rights during the days when women weren't allowed to speak up.

"I would like to be called the Truth," I stated, standing up with perfect posture. "I will not answer to anything else in this house."

Louise raised her eyebrow at me. "The Truth? Now what kind of name is that?"

"It makes a statement," I explained. "You're too young to understand."

"I'm smart," she said. "I study a lot! You make me!"

My sister and I went back and forth making fun of each other's names. After a few seconds we stopped when I heard Vicki's voice from another room, growing louder and louder. I started talking again just so Louise wouldn't be able to hear, but Vicki's voice and tone was clear.

"How am I supposed to pay for that?" she asked angrily. "Where did all our money go?"

"I don't know." My father's deep voice stayed calm.

"I can't live like this!" Vicki yelled.

A chill shot up my spine. *Does she think for one second that we chose for everything to happen this way? Does she think we wanted to live like this?* Sometimes I wanted Vicki to leave our house and never come back. When I heard the door slam, I almost stood up and sang a victory song. But I knew she would be back. Even the strain of all the financial problems my father had from my mother's unpaid medical bills wouldn't keep Vicki away. I didn't understand anything about their relationship.

Just then, Ricki, Johnny, and Blake ran into my room and jumped all over my bed.

"Who said you could come in and disrespect my property like this?" I asked. "Who do you think you are?"

"I'm Johnny," said the five-year-old, giggling.

"I'm Ricki," his three-year-old brother added.

Blake looked at me, and like a true one-year-old, he drooled all over himself. I just shook my head. Our house was a confused mess and those little boys didn't even know it. I wished that I didn't know all about the debts my father owed, how much he didn't like his job, and how much time he spent away from the house to try and make his troubles go away. I thought about the tough times we made it through as a family before Vicki was around. She didn't know what happened. She couldn't understand what it felt like. I watched as her boys giggled and played on the bed. If only I could have felt so free.

I stared out the window and watched a bird fly by. I named off all the different types of birds I knew in alphabetical order. *Bluejay. Canary. Cardinal. Chickadee. Dodo bird. Dove. Eagle. Hummingbird. Loon. Owl. Pigeon. Redbird. Vulture.*

Then the telephone rang and my father called out my name. I ran to the phone and said hello.

"Hi, it's Peaches."

"Hi," I said with a smile. "What's up?"

"How are you getting to Mrs. Ramirez's house?" she asked.

"I'm taking the bus," I said. "You want to go together?"

"Yeah. I'll meet you on the corner of Broadway and Fifth."

I agreed, said goodbye, and hung up the phone. Then I went back to my room and studied for two hours. Louise came in my room several times to ask if I would take her to the O'Malleys'.

"Excuse me, Truth," she said politely. "When can we go? I want to go play in the fort."

I kept telling her "Later, Banana Anna," but she kept

coming back. After the fifth interruption I couldn't take it anymore. I put all my books in my backpack and marched Louise down to the O'Malleys'.

When we arrived, Molly opened the door and Louise eagerly ran inside. "See you later, Truth!" she called out to me.

Molly raised her eyebrows and asked, "Who's Truth?"

"Me," I said proudly. "It's my new nickname."

"Who gave it to you?" she asked.

"I did. I named myself in honor of Sojourner Truth."

"You can't give yourself a nickname," Molly said.

"What rulebook says you can't?" I asked.

"The *How Not to Be a Dork Rulebook*," Molly insisted.

"Never heard of it," I replied.

"You just can't," she said. "Somebody needs to call you a name, and then it sticks."

"Not true. People have called me a lot of names, and I don't answer to them if I don't like them. I like this one."

Molly shook her head. "Fine," she scoffed. "Call yourself Truth. But if anybody asks you why, you can tell them that's what I called you."

"Whatever," I said. "I've got to go. I'm meeting Peaches and we're taking the bus to Mrs. Ramirez's for dinner."

"If you finish before dark, stop by the park," Molly said. "We're playing football. I'll tell everyone your new name."

I grinned proudly.

"See you later, Truth," Molly said, giving me five.

"Thanks, Mo."

I jogged away. Once I realized what I was doing, I slowed down, but I soon started jogging again. I didn't have to run to meet Peaches. I wasn't late. I just couldn't wait to go to see my teammate and teacher. And I was really excited to eat dinner over at someone else's house. I wondered what Mrs. Ramirez was cooking. *Oh, no! I should bring something!* I looked around the neighborhood frantically. A big CLOSED sign hung in the window of the deli. I eyed a huge cake in the window of the bakery. But all the lights were out. It was Sunday and my pockets were empty. I saw Peaches in the distance.

"Hey!" she called out. "How long is the bus ride?"

"It should only take about twelve minutes," I assured her. "Did you bring anything for Mrs. R.?"

"Like what?"

"Like dessert or a house-warming gift?" I asked.

"No, did you?"

I shook my head. "I think we should."

"Do you have any money?" Peaches asked.

"Just enough for the bus," I said.

"Me, too," my friend replied. "Why don't we just say our gift to Mrs. R. will be the Brightest Stars trophy."

I grinned as I imagined what a wonderful gift that would be. Our huge trophy on display in school and then in Mrs. Ramirez's living room. "You're always thinkin', Peach."

As we waited for the bus, I decided to inform my teammate of my new identity.

"Peaches," I said nervously. "I have to tell you something."

"What?"

"I have a new name," I told her.

"A new name?"

"Yeah," I said. "I'm The Truth."

"The what?"

"The Truth," I repeated. "As in Sojourner Truth."

She smiled. "That's cool. Real cool."

"Yeah," I said. "I picked it just for our competition."

"Sounds good to me." Then Peaches added, "Do you think I need a new name, too?"

"Nah, with a name like McCool, what else could you want? Everybody loves your name."

When we arrived at Mrs. Ramirez's house, I could smell the roast in the oven. After I stopped imagining how great dinner would be, all I could think about was whether or not I should tell Mrs. Ramirez my new name. It was my name. I chose it. I wanted people to use it.

"I have a new name for the competition," I stated firmly.

Mrs. Ramirez turned to me. "A new name?" she asked curiously. "What's wrong with Wilma?"

"Nothing," I said. "I just thought I needed something really special for this event."

"Then what is this special name you chose?"

"The Truth," I said. "First name, The, last name, Truth."

Mrs. Ramirez grinned. "Do you think you really need this name?"

"It just feels right for me," I said.

Mrs. Ramirez nodded as she showed us to the table. Then Peaches asked, "What are we working on today?"

"Politics and world history," our teacher said. "We're going to focus on world wars."

"We are?" I gasped. "You didn't tell us that! I only studied U.S. wars. I'm not prepared!"

Mrs. Ramirez looked at me and did not say a word as she waited for me to calm down. For about thirty seconds, my teacher let me panic, ramble, and then apologize.

"Are you ready to start now?" she asked.

I nodded. The three of us reviewed every aspect of the major wars. We discussed both sides of each conflict, the land where the battles were fought, how many lives were lost, the aftermath, and which parties gained or lost control.

Mrs. Ramirez walked over to the oven and peeked inside. I sat up in my seat and my stomach growled. Mr. Ramirez walked in the front door and introduced himself to us. Peaches and I both smiled.

"Dinner is ready," Mrs. Ramirez said. "Would you girls mind clearing the table?"

Five minutes later I was in food heaven with roast beef, mashed potatoes, green beans, and carrot cake for desert. Peaches and I laughed and smiled over the dinner table. It was clear neither of us wanted the meal to end.

After dinner Mrs. Ramirez insisted that we review all the world war questions again. As we studied, I bent my knee and felt my own war wound.

"Ow."

"What's wrong?" Peaches asked me.

"I hurt my knee in volleyball practice," I said.

"How many more games do you have left?" Mrs. Ramirez asked.

"Two this week, two next week, and then one the following week."

"We have a lot of subjects left to cover before the competition," Mrs. Ramirez said. "Do you think you're going to be able to handle all of this with volleyball?"

"Sure," I said confidently. "I've been doing this for years. Don't sweat it, Mrs. R."

"The Truth can get the job done," Peaches announced.

I smiled and gave her a high five.

After we finished studying and entertaining our teacher, we thanked her and said goodbye.

"See you tomorrow!" she said.

Peaches and I rode the bus back home together. By the end of the short ride, I really had to use the bathroom. "Can I stop at your house to use the bathroom?" I asked as we stepped off the bus.

"Sure," she said. "My mom is working, but my brother is home."

When we arrived at Peaches' house, she pushed open the door, and my eyes stopped on a boy in a wheelchair.

"This is Smooth," Peaches said. "Smooth, this is The Truth."

The boy waved his hand and half-smiled. Peaches had never told me about her brother.

"Hi," I said. "What's your real name?"

"Smooth." He gave me a thumbs-up sign.

"No, it's not," Peaches said with a grin. "It's Randy. I nicknamed him Smooth a while ago because I didn't like to call him Randy. That was my father's name. He left us just after Smooth was born. I was three. Haven't seen him since."

A dreadful moment of silence passed. "Oh," I muttered nervously. "Where'd you say the bathroom was?"

"Down the hall," she said.

I hustled down the hallway and into the bathroom. Shutting the door, I took a good, long look at myself in the mirror. I wondered if Peaches could tell how surprised I was about her brother. I wondered why she told me so much about her family's problems. *Isn't that private information?*

I finished in the bathroom and walked back to the living room. When I saw Peaches, I felt an urge to tell her about my mother. Maybe it was because she didn't know me that well outside of school. I was always afraid to talk about my mother with the Ballplayers because they had known her. We were all so close and the memories hurt so much. If I started to tell the Ballplayers how I felt about my mother, I would start to cry and never be able to stop.

But my emotions felt safe with Peaches. Maybe I would be able to tell her and be okay with it. *What will I say? How do I begin? I can't tell her everything. I can't tell her about how I didn't cry at my mother's funeral. She won't understand. No one will.*

I looked up at the wall and saw a framed picture of Dr. Martin Luther King, Jr. I immediately started to recite one of my favorite parts of his "I Have a Dream" speech.

"I have a dream that my four little children will one day live in a nation where they will not be judged by the color of their skin but by the content of their character."

"I have a dream today!" Peaches called out.

We smiled as we spoke loud and true. There was no stopping us. I tucked all my sad thoughts away and thought about one thing: winning the Brightest Stars competition.

Chapter 6

My father was staring down at the newspaper as I walked into the kitchen that night.

"Hi, Dad," I said, hoping to at least get a smile out of him. I knew how upset Vicki was. I really wanted to ask him how he put up with all of her nonsense.

When he didn't respond, I tried again.

"How was your day?" I asked.

His tired eyes finally looked at me, and I grinned like an Olympic Gold Medalist.

"Fine," he said. "Where have you been?"

"Remember? I told you that I was going over to Mrs. Ramirez's house with Peaches?" I asked.

"Who's Peaches?"

My shoulders drooped and I huffed. "You know, Dad. The girl I study with all the time."

"Oh, that's right," he said.

I sat down next to him and opened up the business section of the newspaper and started reading.

"I didn't know you read the business section," he said.

"Yeah. I'm thinking of being a stockbroker someday." I pulled that one out of the air, but it sure sounded good. "Either that or a financial analyst," I added.

"I thought you wanted to be a lawyer?" he asked.

"In my spare time I thought I'd do some serious investing," I said.

My dad just shook his head, and then he smiled. I grinned like a three-time Olympic Gold Medalist.

"Do you have any basketball games this week?" my father asked.

I just shook my head. Sometimes my father and I would be standing in the same room, but it felt as if we were miles and miles away. It hadn't taken me long to figure out that the combination of my mother's absence and his tedious factory job really gave my father the bluest of blues. It all started when he and his partner bought and worked on a large plot of land in the country. Actually my father did all the work, and his partner did all the instructing.

Then two big businessmen with a lot of money came by and made a huge offer to buy the land. I remember the day my dad came home and told us about the deal. He ran into the house and then straight into the bedroom where my mother was resting. He dropped down to his knees and told her that we would get half of the money. She smiled, laughed, and became stronger every day that week. I believed we finally had Lady Luck in our corner, and so did my father. This mighty miracle would cure my mother and make us live happily ever after.

But when my father arrived on his piece of land the next day and tried to get into his tiny office, the door was bolted. The two businessmen showed up and said they now owned the place. My father tried to call his partner, but the man's phone line was disconnected. He called all of his partner's family and friends. Nobody could find him. Within days my father found out that his partner had taken all the money and run out of town.

The worst part about the whole story was when my father came home at the end of that week. I looked at him and could see that he had been crying. He never told my mother about what happened. He just kept telling her that the deal was almost done. It wasn't the money that had made them happy. It was the hope that good things could still happen to our family. He didn't want to let that go.

My mother passed away two months later.

The saddest part was that my mother went to her grave believing that her family would have a better life than when she was alive. Even when she reached heaven, I still didn't want her to know the truth of how that man cheated our family at a time when my dad felt robbed of his wife, and Lou-Lou and I felt robbed of our mother.

"It's *volleyball* season, Dad," I said.

"I'm sorry. That's what I meant. You should write your schedule down and post it on the refrigerator. I'm going to try to make it to one of your games."

I was thrilled that he was actually interested. "Really?" I said.

He nodded.

"I'm the star player," I said, jumping up from my seat. "I can bump, set, spike, and man-oh-man I can serve with the best of 'em!" I demonstrated every move, and then I quickly ran into my room to get my volleyball for my dad. I started to show him offenses and defenses.

"This is the middle hitter," I pointed out. "This is the setter."

In the middle of our conversation Vicki and the boys barged into the room, laughing and yelling.

"What are you doing?" Johnny asked.

"Nothing," I said. I closed my book, left the table, and accepted that the quality time I had spent with my father was over. It was time to study by myself. Louise skipped through the doorway and followed me right into my bedroom.

"Go get me the paper," I said as I sat down on my bed. "I forgot to check something."

"What's the magic word?" Louise asked.

I rolled my eyes. "Please, Shorty."

Louise left and returned with a load of newspapers in her arms.

"Here," she said, dropping the papers on my bed. "And no more calling me Shorty."

"Thanks," I said. "Where's the horoscope page?"

"What's a horoscope?"

"It's something that predicts your future," I explained. "It has to do with astrology."

"What's astrology?" she asked.

"It's all in the stars," I said as I flipped through the pages. "Ah! Here it is!"

You continue to light up a room with your glowing personality. You finally get a golden opportunity this week to overcome adversity and establish yourself as a bright and shining star.

"Yes!" I called out. "I'm going to be the star this week! I just know it! This says my chance is finally here! I can't wait!" I reached out my hand and said, "Hey! Hey! What do you say?" Louise and I slapped each other with a double high five.

"What does it say about me?" Louise asked.

"Let me check," I said. "Here it is."

If you study hard in school and treat your sister like a queen you will get a big reward at the end of the week.

All right, yeah, I made it up. But Louise loved it.

"A reward!" she gasped. "Really?"

"Sure," I said.

"What kind of reward?"

"I don't know," I replied. I'd figure that out later.

"How nice do I have to be to my sister?" she asked.

"Super nice or else no reward."

"I'm going to check over all my homework," she said as she hurried out of the room.

I settled down in my chair and couldn't let go of my volleyball book. I cherished every second of the conversation about volleyball I had with my dad. I decided to write down a list of things I would do in practice the next day.

RUN A LOT
HUSTLE
ENCOURAGE OTHERS
NOT GET INTO TROUBLE WITH MOLLY
TELL COACH KIM WHAT A WONDERFUL
   HUMAN BEING SHE IS

After rereading my list, I crossed out the last sentence. I didn't need to try and flatter Coach Kim for playing time. I would just show her what she'd been missing all year in her starting line-up. A player with pizzazz. Gumption. Desire. Determination. I did 10 jumping jacks and 10 deep knee bends. Then I felt a shot of pain in my knee. *I forgot to ice!* I ran to the refrigerator and stuffed a bunch of ice in an empty plastic bread bag. Then I limped back to my room and rested the ice on my knee as I settled in with my vocabulary list. But I couldn't get my mind off volleyball and how great I would perform the very next day.

After all, I had told my father I was the superstar, and The Truth couldn't lie.

Chapter 7

The next morning I walked down the stairs and out the front door. I looked up and saw Molly dragging herself down the sidewalk.

"Good morning, Sunshine!" I shouted.

Molly glared at me and rolled her eyes. She didn't usually speak a full sentence until after ten A.M.

"You look so lovely this morning!" I said.

"Cut it out, Wil."

"You look fabulous, darling, just fabulous!" I continued.

"Wil!" Molly warned. "I'm not in the mood, all right?"

I kept talking and joking around. Molly just ignored me. When we walked down Broadway and turned the corner of Woodside, Molly suddenly burst out laughing. I turned and looked at her and her eyes were locked on the Drill Sergeant's house.

71

"Look at that!" she said in a loud whisper. "Look at him! He must have locked his keys inside!"

I almost fell over laughing. This was just too good to be true. Shawn Plumley, whom we had nicknamed the Drill Sergeant, had been the number-one target of our pranks and jokes. We had also been his favorite kids to chase around the neighborhood.

I grinned at the hilarious sight of his back end and legs sticking out the tiny window of his truck. The Drill Sergeant was totally helpless. Molly and I laughed so hard that my insides hurt.

"Shhh!" Molly said. "Shhh! He'll hear us!"

The Drill Sergeant slowly twisted and wiggled his way out of the window.

"I wish I had a camera!" I said. "This is great!"

Once he landed on his feet, the Drill Sergeant turned and looked straight at us. I wanted to run.

"Let's go," I muttered nervously.

But Molly didn't move.

"I guess we should help," she said, and she started walking over.

"What?" I exclaimed. "Are you crazy?"

"He needs some help," she said.

"I thought you couldn't stand the guy?" I asked.

"I can't. But maybe it's time to call a truce."

I raced up next to her. "What has gotten into you all of a sudden?"

"He needs some help," Molly said. "One of us can fit in that window better than he can."

"Oh, yeah, right. With whose body?" I said, looking from my body to Molly's.

"I can fit," Molly said.

"No, you can't."

"What are you trying to say?" Molly said. "It's not like *you* could fit."

"And I'm not ashamed to admit it," I agreed. "They'd need the jaws of life to get me outta there."

I looked at Shawn Plumley and didn't know what to do, but I was not about to let stubborn Molly O'Malley crawl in that back window. When she jumped up in the bed of the truck, I yelled, "I'm going to get your mom before you hurt yourself."

I turned away and saw petite Rosie Jones jogging straight at us. "Ro's here!" I said. "She'll do it!" I whistled and waved Rosie over. "We need you, Ro!"

Rosie jumped up, crawled into the truck, grabbed the keys, climbed out, and tossed them to Shawn Plumley.

"That's my girl!" I said. "Way to go, Ro!"

Rosie jumped off the truck and readjusted her baseball cap.

"Thanks," the Drill Sergeant said.

"Don't mention it," I said. "We care about our neighborhood."

As we walked away, I couldn't believe what we had just done. Being on friendly terms with one of our archrivals felt strange.

"That makes up for the time I threw the tennis ball into his house," Rosie whispered.

"But what about when he let that dog chase us around the neighborhood?" I asked.

"He's still a little strange," Molly said. "But it wouldn't be any fun if we stopped bugging him."

The Broadway Ballplayers

The little things we did to the Drill Sergeant weren't mean and rotten. But the kids at school that day were. The ambush started the minute I walked in the front door of Lincoln School.

"Did you do your social studies homework?" Eddie asked.

I simply ignored him, disgusted that he actually thought I'd hand my homework over to him.

"Didn't anyone ever teach you how to share?" he asked.

I stared straight ahead in silence.

"What's the big deal?" he continued. "It's homework. A piece of paper. Who cares?"

I started humming a song. Eddie's face turned beat red.

"Just give me the homework," he barked.

I felt my anger rise inside of me. "Do you even have a brain?" I asked.

"You're really funny, Wil," he muttered.

"No," I said. "I'm serious. You think I'm really dumb enough to give you my homework?"

"Just one time wouldn't hurt you."

"No," I said. "I give it to you once, and the next thing I know, you'll be coming to me for your homework like you go after Billy for his lunch money. Not a chance."

"Fine, fat girl," he said.

Eddie was missing a heart along with his brain. He didn't care how much he humiliated people.

"You're such a—" I began.

I stopped speaking just as Mr. Gordon turned the corner. I turned to Eddie, stood up straight, and grinned.

"Eddie is bugging me, Mr. G.!" I blurted out.

"What's the problem?" the principal asked.

Out of the corner of my eye, I could see Eddie glaring at me. If I told Mr. G. that Eddie had tried to copy my homework, Eddie would torture me for eternity.

"I've tried to ignore him," I explained. "I really tried to walk away. I've practiced all the things you taught us: patience, fairness, and peace. But I'm going to slug him in about thirty seconds."

"Eddie," Mr. Gordon said. "Go have a seat in my office."

I grinned like a champ. Eddie scowled. "I didn't do anything!" he shouted. "You always believe everybody else. You never believe me!"

"Eddie," Mr. Gordon stated firmly. "We'll talk about it in my office. Let's go."

Eddie strutted down the hallway, shaking his head.

"Are you all right?" Mr. G. asked me.

"I'm under so much stress," I said, "I think I might be getting an ulcer."

"Have you been studying a lot?"

I nodded. "But that's not what's bugging me."

"What is it, then?"

"Coach Kim doesn't play me," I said. "I'm good, Mr. G. I should be playing!"

Mr. Gordon sighed. "There will always be others who don't think you can do something. You can choose to listen to those who say you can't, or you can focus on all those who believe in you."

"It's not that easy."

He smiled. "Who said it was easy?"

"Thanks, Mr. G.," I said, then I turned to walk away.

"One quick question," he called out. "What's this about you changing your name to the Truth for the competition? Aren't you proud of being Wil?"

"Yes. But I want to be big-time. I need a great name that people won't forget."

Mr. G. shook his head. "All right," he said. "But when you become famous, will I have to call you Miss Thomas?"

"Wil is fine," I said. "And don't worry, Mr. G. I won't forget you."

Our school principal grinned as he walked away. Now that he had Eddie under control, I thought my peer pressure problems were over. But when I walked into our classroom, two of my classmates glared at me. "I heard you went over to Mrs. Ramirez's house yesterday for dinner," one said. "Now we all know why you get straight *A*s."

I didn't even attempt to explain myself.

"What's it like being teacher's pet?" another said.

"Who would want to be a square anyway?" a third muttered.

I looked up at Mrs. Ramirez and gave her a big smile. Then I turned back to my jealous classmates and grinned. "Maybe we can study together sometime?" I said.

They all glared at me. I smiled and turned to Peaches. "What's up, girl?"

"I'm all right. What's up with you?"

"I just got Eddie sent to the office," I said proudly, expecting her to laugh and give me a high five.

Peaches didn't smile. She looked up at the blackboard and took down some notes. "I didn't get to study much last night."

"Why not?" I asked.

"My brother isn't feeling very well."

"Oh," I said softly. "Is he going to be okay?"

"We don't know," Peaches said as her eyes drifted off in the distance. My heart ached in my chest. I knew exactly how she felt. "I'll tell you about it later," she added.

After my third class that day I ran into Coach Kim in the hallway.

"I just want to let you know I am really excited about practice today," I said proudly, showing off my best possible attitude.

"Great," she said. "When is that academic competition you're in?"

"Approximately eleven days and twenty-three hours," I said. "One week from this coming Saturday at nine A.M. sharp. But don't worry. I'm not going to miss any practice or games."

"Sounds like you and Peaches have a good chance to win," Coach Kim said.

"Yeah . . . Did I tell you how excited I am about practice today?"

"Yes, you did," she said, smiling. "I'll see you after school."

I ran into the locker room at two forty-five P.M., changed like Superwoman, and then rushed into the gym.

"Why are you in such a hurry?" Molly asked.

"I want to be one of the first players in the gym," I answered. I stretched out, warmed up, and put on my mean, intense, serious game face.

"Wil," Penny said.

I ignored her and kept my focus.

"Wil," Penny repeated.

"What?" I shot back, irritated by the interruption.

"Your shorts are on backward."

I looked down and sighed. The whistle blew and Coach Kim screamed, "Let's get going, girls!"

I looked down again at my shorts and then at my coach, hoping she wouldn't notice. I couldn't risk being late by running back into the locker room and turning them around. Every second counted with Coach Kim.

"You've got your shorts on backward," Molly whispered.

"I know," I muttered. "I know!"

"Wil!" Coach Kim screamed. "Please control your mouth today!"

"I didn't do anything," I pleaded.

"Five laps and ten push-ups for talking when I was talking."

I started into a jog and then rushed into a mad sprint. *This isn't fair! I'm going to show Coach Kim! I'm going to show her!* After completing my punishment, I raced back on to the court and joined my team in a defensive drill. I waited my turn, and when it came, I adjusted my glasses and clapped my hands.

"I can do this!" I yelled, trying to pump myself up.

Coach Kim slammed the ball at me. I hit it. In the wrong direction. She slammed the next, and I hit that one too. Right into the net.

"You got it, Truth!" Molly said. "Stick with it!"

I hung in there and hit the next two passes as if I had written the volleyball manual myself. At the end of the drill I reached out and made everyone give me a high five. Coach Kim blew her whistle and called out, "Agility and speed drills."

So soon?

"Put fifteen minutes on the clock!" she hollered. Our manager rushed over to the clock and hit a few buttons. My mouth fell open. I turned to everyone on my team, but they were just shaking their heads.

"What is she doing?" I asked. "This is way too early to be doing the pass-out drills."

"No talking!" Coach Kim warned.

My eyes bulged. I had narrowly escaped another punishment. I had to pull myself together. Like a true champion, I told myself to strap on the task and get the job done. I ran, jumped, and sprinted for fifteen minutes straight. When time ran out, I cheered like a fool.

Then Coach Kim put another fifteen minutes on the clock.

"She should be fired for this," I grumbled. "Somebody had better turn her in."

"Is there a problem, Wil?" Coach Kim yelled.

"No," I replied. "This is my favorite drill."

I thought if I said it was my favorite, I would believe it myself. But I didn't. At the eight-minute mark I collapsed. My lungs overworked themselves. Once I dropped to the ground, I had no desire or energy to get up.

"You got too excited before practice," Molly advised after practice.

"Yeah," Penny added. "You've got to chill out. Relax. you're too stressed."

"Maybe I should see a psychologist," I said, being dramatic.

"No," Molly said. "Just take a night off. Don't study tonight."

"It's not the Stars competition," I admitted. "It's volleyball. Not playing is driving me crazy. It's taking over my whole life, and I don't know what to do about it."

"Talk to Coach Kim," Molly suggested.

"Yeah, right. I'd have better luck talking to the wall."

"Just stick with it," Penny added. "Don't give up."

"I didn't say anything about giving up," I said defensively.

Penny and Molly looked at each other and just shook their heads.

"I'm sorry," I said. "I'm sorry for snapping at you. I've got to get through this. I can do it."

I gave myself a pep talk the whole way home. Over and over I told myself the same things. *I'm intelligent, athletic, strong, good-looking. I believe in myself! I'm the best. I'm number one. I am the Truth!*

I walked in the door and Louise greeted me.

"Hi, Truth," she said.

"What's up, Banana Anna?" I asked.

I dropped my books off in my room, and Lou-Lou followed me in. I looked on my shelf and pulled out a book on CPR.

"What's that book about?" Lou-Lou asked.

"Cardiopulmonary resuscitation," I said.

"Huh?" she asked.

"CPR," I said. "It's done to save a person's life. I want to learn how to do this so I can save a person's life someday."

"I want to save one, too!" Lou-Lou said.

The phone rang. I jumped up, bumped my knee, and limped to the receiver.

"Hello?" I said.

"Hi, Wil," a voice said. "This is Peaches. What are you doing?"

"I'm studying CPR," I said.

"You are?" she asked.

"Yeah," I said.

"Why?"

"Because if we lose this competition," I said, "you might have to bring me back to life."

"Oh," Peaches said. "That's kind of why I called."

"What's wrong?" I asked.

"It's my brother," she said. "His brain tumor is getting worse. We have to drive a long way to get him to the best hospital."

"Oh, no." My eyes began to water. "Is he going to be all right?"

"I think so," she said. "Smooth likes it when I go with him. I've got to go with him tomorrow, and I don't know how long it will be before I'm back."

"Is it that bad?" I asked.

"I'm not sure," she said. "But I just wanted to let you know that I checked in the rules, and you can compete in the competition all by yourself. You don't need me to win. If I can't make it, I know you still can win for our school. I know you can do it."

"But, Peaches—"

"Don't worry about me," she said. "I'll call you and let you know what's happening. I've gotta go. Good luck."

The phone clicked and Peaches was gone. I was sad and scared for Smooth. I thought about my mother. I didn't want Smooth to go through all the pain and suffering. I wanted everything to work out and all the pain to go away. My legs started to feel weak. I went back to my room and lay down on the bed.

Chapter 8

I rushed into my classroom the next morning, dropped my books on my desk, and went straight up to my teacher.

"How am I supposed to do this all by myself?" my voice cracked. "I can't do this without Peaches!"

"Relax, Wil," Mrs. Ramirez said soothingly. "Settle down."

I felt the sweat trickle down my face as I looked around the room. Everyone was staring at me.

I rushed out of the room and down the hall. I pushed open the rest room door and hid in the stall.

After a few minutes a voice called out, "Wil, is that you?"

It was Penny. I did not say a word.

"I know you're in here," she said.

"You almost knocked over three people," Molly added.

"I did?" I gasped. "Sorry."

"What's wrong?" Penny asked.

"Eighth grade stinks," I said from behind the closed door. "Enjoy every minute of seventh grade because when you get in eighth, the real world hits and it's tough. It's really, really tough."

"It can't be that bad," Penny said.

I wiped my eyes with my sleeve and then readjusted my glasses. Taking a deep breath, I came out of my hiding spot, just as Mrs. Ramirez walked into the girls' room.

"Penny and Molly, back to your rooms," she said.

My friends hustled out. The door slammed shut, leaving me alone with my teacher. Her face was red. I could see the veins in her neck bulging.

"You had better not feel sorry for yourself for one second!" she said. "After working so hard, you have to do this. You owe it to me. You owe it to Peaches, and, above all, you owe it to yourself."

"Peaches must be so upset," I started. "Is her brother going to be all right?"

"We don't know," Mrs. Ramirez said.

"I don't want to have to go through this," I mumbled.

"She is strong, Wil. Just like you."

A group of girls rushed into the room, and I wiped my tears again.

"Let's get back to class," Mrs. Ramirez said.

I followed my teacher out of the room, and we bumped into Coach Kim.

Sideline Blues by Wil

"Good morning," Coach Kim greeted us.

"Hi," Mrs. Ramirez said. "When is the next game?"

"Today," I replied enthusiastically. I wanted to leave Coach Kim with a good impression. She had to know how much I wanted to play. "It's a home game."

"That's right," Coach Kim said. "I'll see you after school, Wil. Be ready."

"You can count on it!" I yelled as she continued down the hallway with her back to me. "I am Miss Ready. Miss Prepared. Miss Volleyball. That's me! You just wait and see!"

Coach Kim kept walking and didn't even smile or nod when I shouted out the cheers for myself. Then Mrs. Ramirez turned to me. "Are you sure you can still handle both volleyball and the competition?" she asked. "I'm sure Coach Kim would understand if it's too much."

"I can do it," I assured her. "Coach Kim doesn't know it yet, but I'm going to have a huge game today."

My forecast of my volleyball performance almost carried me through school the entire day. But during my last class, Mrs. Ramirez gave me a list of subjects to study for the competition and I almost passed out.

The Industrial Revolution
Plants and Animals
Famous Artists
Famous Places

"I haven't reviewed any of this!" I said.

"Peaches was covering these subjects. Now it's up to you."

85

I moaned in frustration. Mrs. Ramirez rested her hand on my shoulder.

"The more I give you," my teacher said, "the more you will get done. Call me tonight if you have any questions," she added.

When the last bell rang, I loaded my arms full of books, jogged out of the classroom, and turned the corner.

"Hey, fat girl," Eddie called out. "Are those too heavy for you?"

I turned and scowled at the creep. "Shut up, fat head!" I shouted out. As I turned away, I missed a step and tripped. I couldn't catch myself and I hit the floor. My knee slammed against the tiles and I screamed. I held my breath and felt all the anger and pain rush through my body. "You . . . you . . ?" I screamed at Eddie.

Then Mr. Gordon's eyes stared down at me. I wondered if he had heard me call Eddie "fat head." Mr. G. didn't tolerate name-calling. But I didn't care. Eddie made me so mad. He had no right to say anything about my body. It wasn't his. It was mine. I never mentioned his short legs and arms. I didn't make comments about his skinny neck even though it made him look like a snake.

"Are you okay?" Mr. G. asked.

I didn't even speak. I couldn't. I was so mad that I knew I was about to cry, and I would not, could not have an emotional breakdown in front of Eddie Thompson. I took slow deep breaths. Penny and Molly walked up and helped me limp off to the nurse's office.

"It was all Eddie's fault, Mr. G.," Molly said. "I saw it!"

Mr. G. ignored her. Instead he put his arm over Eddie and marched him down the hall. As we limped into the office, Nurse Carol turned and looked at me. I burst into tears.

"My knee!" I complained. "It hurts so bad."

"It's okay, Wil," she said. "Just relax. Penny and Molly, go and get ready for your game."

"I've got to be able to play!" I said. "They need me!"

"Take care of yourself, Truth," Molly said.

My friends left the room, and I made myself stop crying. There was no time to feel sorry for myself. I had to get better in a hurry. My fate lay in Nurse Carol's hands. She pulled out a pack of ice and a bandage. I loved ice. Just the sight of it made me feel better.

"I want you to wear two knee pads on this knee today for extra protection."

"I will," I said gratefully. "I will. I promise."

With every minute I felt more confident of my chances for healing.

"When is that competition you're in?" Nurse Carol asked.

"Next weekend," I said. "I'm in it all by myself."

Nurse Carol looked up at the clock. "You're going to be late."

I had exactly five minutes and thirty-three seconds to be in the gym in full uniform. I carried my bag of ice as I limped out of the office and turned at the door.

"Are you coming to the game?" I asked.

"Maybe," Nurse Carol said.

"Are you coming to the academic competition next week?"

"I'm going to try," she said as she glanced at the clock. "You'd better hurry up."

I ran down the hall and into the locker room. I talked to everyone around me as I took off my clothes and put on my uniform.

"We're going to win today," I said. "I just know it. I feel it."

Nobody said anything.

"What's the matter with everyone?" I asked.

"You're going to be late," a teammate said. "And we're all going to be in trouble."

"I'm not going to be late," I said. "I'm never late."

I stuck my sneaker into the leg hole in my shorts and it got stuck. I tried to wiggle out of it, but then I heard a rip.

"Oh, no!" I said. "Anybody have an extra pair of shorts?"

Most of my teammates had already left the locker room.

"Will somebody help me?" I asked. "Somebody tell Penny!"

I started to sweat bullets as I looked at the clock. I had thirty seconds to be out on the floor, and I was standing in my underwear. I couldn't be late. I couldn't! I wrapped a towel around my waist and burst through the locker room doors.

"What are you doing?" Molly yelled when she saw me in my towel.

"I ripped my shorts," I said. "This is all I have."

Penny rushed toward me. "Get back in there before Coach Kim sees you."

"I'm going to be late!" I said. "If I'm late, we're all going to have to run."

Penny pushed me into the locker room. I followed

behind her and looked down at my towel. I realized that I looked ridiculous.

"Here," Penny said, throwing me a pair of fifth-grade shorts.

"These are too small," I said. "I can't fit into these."

"Put 'em on," Penny said. "Hurry up."

I squeezed each leg into the shorts and followed Penny out the door. Coach Kim was waiting. By her icy stare, I knew that then was not the time to ask for an extra knee pad.

"What has taken so long?" she asked.

"My shorts ripped," Penny said.

I looked at Penny and my eyes grew wide. I couldn't believe that she would take the fall for this one. Coach Kim thought Penny walked on water.

"You're late; we run," Coach Kim said.

She rounded us all up and ran us through the pass-out drills. I couldn't believe she didn't let it slide. *Are you crazy? We have a game to play!*

The referee blew the whistle to start the game, and I called out, "Thank you!" I had never been so happy to hear a whistle in my life.

"Let's go, Lincoln," the referee called out. "I need the starters on the floor."

I looked at Coach Kim and grinned. She just glanced at her clipboard and called out the starters. "Anita, Molly, Penny, Jozette, Sam, and Amy."

I grabbed a towel and pretended to blot my face. I closed my eyes and fought my tears.

"What's the matter?" a teammate asked me. "You got the blues?"

"Yeah," I said. "I've got the blues."

I took a deep breath and with what little strength I had, I added a verse to my song.

> *Before I walk out that door,*
> *I just want one chance*
> *to get out on that floor.*

My teammates laughed. I turned to Coach Kim, but she hadn't heard me. All she saw and heard were the starters. I sat on the bench and rubbed my knee. She didn't know the pain I overcame for the sake of the team.

"Wil," Coach Kim called out after a while. "Go in for Amy."

I jumped up, screamed, "Yes, baby! Yes!" and ran to my spot on the floor. Out of the corner of my eye I saw Nurse Carol. *She is here! She is watching me! I'm going to show her how great I am!* Then I looked down at my knee. *Oh, no! I forgot my extra knee pad!*

"Pay attention, Wil!" Coach Kim called out.

I looked through the net and watched the server wind up. She smacked the ball over the net, and I breathed a huge sigh of relief when it didn't come flying right at me. We volleyed back and forth for a few hits and then the ball fell in my territory. I lined myself up under it and smacked it solid. I grinned when the ball traveled to our setter, exactly where I planned on sending it. It was perfect, the best bump I'd ever seen. Penny spiked the set over the net and we scored. I jumped up and down and high-fived every player on my team. Everybody cheered.

"Yeah, P.!"

"Way to go, Sweet P.!"

"Nice one, Penny!"

I looked around and waited for everyone to cheer for me. Penny couldn't have hit that ball if it weren't for my perfect bump. *What about me?*

On the next play the ball came to me again, and I set it up perfectly again. I was good. Really good. I glanced over at my coach to make sure she was watching. She was. I turned back to the game, and the ball came to me again. I hit it. I hadn't made a single mistake in three hits. I was playing well. Really, really well. My knee throbbed, but I fought through the agony. I imagined the whole crowd rooting wildly for me. I envisioned my sister and my father leading the pack. Lou-Lou held a sign up that said, "The Truth is #1! You can't stop her. She's the best!" I blushed. They all grabbed pens and pieces of paper so I could sign autographs after the game. *I should be an all-star. I should be player of the game!*

I would have been the player of the day if the other team hadn't started its comeback so soon. Point by point they rallied and then went up by two. None of the mistakes were my fault, but I started to sweat. I danced around in my spot and encouraged my team.

"We can do it!" I said. "Let's stay together. Stay focused. Be strong. Play the game. Keep your cool."

"Wil!" Coach Kim screamed. "Stop talking and pay attention!"

They need me! Let me cheer! Then a flying object hit me in the stomach. It was the volleyball. The other team roared as they won the game. I fell down on the floor and put my hand out so I wouldn't fall on my bad knee. All of my weight came down on my right wrist.

"Ow!" I screamed.

Nobody came running. After a few seconds I stood up and moped over to the sideline. For the next game Coach Kim said, "Wil's out, Amy's back in."

I wanted to cry, so I grabbed the towel and blotted my face again. Coach Kim kept me on the bench for the rest of the match. I took a long look across the gym and wondered how I would feel if I walked across the floor, out the door, and never came back.

Chapter 9

After the game I stomped out of the gym.

"What's wrong?" Penny asked.

I rolled my eyes. "What do you think?" I asked sarcastically. "You try sitting on the bench all year and see how your butt feels."

"You're probably not going to listen to me, but I'll say it anyway," she said. "We need you."

"For what?" I asked. "Coach Kim doesn't let me do anything."

"You help," Penny said. "You work hard and care about us."

"Is that all I do?" I asked.

"You make things fun," she added with a smile.

"What else?" I asked.

Penny paused and then her eyes grew wide. "You're

smart," she added. "And when you win the Brightest Stars competition you'll be famous."

I grinned proudly.

"Now can I stop telling you how great you are?" Penny asked.

"Yes," I said, feeling better. "That's enough for now. Thanks."

Penny shook her head and laughed. I kept smiling, thinking of all the nice things she had said about me.

"So what's up with Peaches?" Penny asked. "I heard her brother is sick."

"That's all I know," I told my friend.

"Are you going to be all right without her?"

"Yeah, I guess," I replied. "I'm just really worried about Smooth."

As I walked up Broadway Avenue, I couldn't shake off my thoughts of him and his family. When I opened the door to our apartment, I said hi to Vicki and the boys and then I went straight to my room. I buried my head in my pillow, but told myself that I would not cry. I hated to cry because I never cried at my mother's funeral. There. I said it. I never cried at my mother's funeral. Whenever I cried I thought about how I couldn't when I should have been crying. I was ashamed of myself for a long time. I just didn't know what to do. I wanted to cry, but I was afraid. I didn't want to believe my mother had left us for good. I had my mind made up that she would be back.

It wasn't until about a year later that I accepted that my mother wasn't coming back. I saw my father cry a few times, but he always tried to hide his tears with a pair of sunglasses or the brim of his hat. Seeing him hide his tears and emotions made me do the same. My friends tried to get me to talk about how I was feeling, but I was too scared to say anything. I didn't think I was allowed to talk about it.

As I thought of Eddie calling me "fat girl," more tears welled in my eyes. I hated when he said that. No matter how badly cancer had torn up her body, my mother never once complained about how she looked. Even with her hair falling out and her body shrinking to skin and bones, she never once held her head down in shame. She was just as strong at 90 pounds as she had been at 180.

In sixth grade I realized that I missed my mother more than I did when I was in fifth. And in seventh grade I missed her more than I did when I was in sixth. Now I was in eighth grade, and I wanted her to be there every second of the day to help me with every decision. At that moment I wanted her to tell me what I could say or do that would make Smooth and Peaches feel better. I wanted my mother to stroke my hair gently with her hand and plant a soft kiss on my forehead. She would tell me that everything was going to be okay, and I would believe her.

I rolled over in my bed and told myself to stop thinking so much. I didn't want my mother to think I was mad at her for not being there. It wasn't her fault. I recalled all of her exciting plans to finish her college education. She had cut back her work schedule so she could take classes at night for her degree. She wanted to be a grade-school principal. She said it would take her years of night school to accomplish her dream. Our family scraped by to pay the rent and bills just so we could have a better future someday. That someday for my mother never came. I felt my skin grow hot and the tears flow down my cheeks. *Why am I still so down? I'm in eighth grade now, I'm supposed to be growing up! Why am I so scared?* I looked up at the ceiling and told my mother about all my worries, and I imagined what she would say.

"Don't be scared. Here is your chance. Go for your dream!"

My mother used to get up every morning and sit with Lou-Lou and me at the breakfast table and tell us how proud she was of us for doing so well in school. It was during second grade that I noticed how tired she was all the time. The doctors didn't diagnose her disease until nine months later. By then the cancer had spread through her entire body, and there wasn't any stopping it. The doctors tried their best with all the radiation and chemotherapy treatments, which seemed to make my mother sicker. The tumors were spreading too fast for any medicine to stop. Within months she couldn't work, eat, or sleep, and she certainly could not take care of us. So I started taking care of her. Feeding her. Reading to her. Playing games. I did laundry and picked up the house. Even at her weakest moments she always took our hands and gave us a kiss. Then she would tell us, "Be all you can be today!" I knew that every day when I walked out that door for school, I was getting an education for two people: me and my mother.

I got tired of sitting around and feeling sad, so I

jumped up from my bed and started cleaning my room. I organized my new library books on my bookshelf alphabetically by author. Then I sharpened all my pencils. I opened up my bottom desk drawer and pulled out all of my files and started studying. I called out my answers and gave myself high fives. I imagined myself on the winner's stand giving a victory speech. *Should I make a list of all the people I have to thank? Nah, that would be too arrogant. I am not arrogant. I'm confident. Assertive. I can do this! Can I do this? What about Peaches? It won't be the same without her. It won't mean anything unless she is there and her brother is okay.*

I couldn't take the anxiety anymore. I picked up the phone book, flipped open the yellow pages to Hospitals, and grabbed a slip of paper. One by one I started calling.

"Randy McCool's room, please," I said, being sure to use Randy's real name.

Nobody had a Randy McCool. I tried one hospital after another. After five tries, I slammed the phone down. My eyes and hands searched frantically for more hospitals. When I ran out, I called information for more numbers.

I had to talk to Peaches.

Chapter 10

Mrs. Ramirez didn't come to school the next day until after lunch. With one class left I finally spotted her walking down the hall. I sprinted through the hallway and caught up with my favorite teacher.

"Where have you been all day?" I asked impatiently.

"I had a doctor's appointment this morning," she replied.

"I've been waiting for you all day."

"What's wrong?" she asked.

"I'm going to see Peaches and Smooth."

Mrs. Ramirez sighed. "The hospital is a good three hours away. Will your father let you go?"

I clasped my hands and begged. "Please help me. Please!"

"I don't think it's a good idea for you to go to the

hospital," she said. "That's a place for the family right now."

I stomped my foot on the ground like my little sister always did when she didn't get her way.

"I think you should call her," Mrs. Ramirez said. "That would be nice."

I whipped out my list of hospitals and showed it to my teacher. "These are all the ones I called and this is what they said."

"When did you do this?" she asked.

"Last night."

"No wonder you look so tired," she told me. "You were supposed to be studying."

"I couldn't concentrate," I said. "I'm worried about Peaches and her family."

"We all are," my teacher agreed. "Come with me and we'll try calling them."

I jumped up right behind my teacher and followed her down the hallway. We stopped in Nurse Carol's office. Mrs. Ramirez and Nurse Carol whispered for a minute, then Mrs. Ramirez told me to come in. She picked up the phone and dialed a number.

"McCool," she said into the receiver. Then she waited. I held my breath. Five seconds passed. Then ten. Then twenty. I gasped for air.

"What?" I asked frantically as Mrs. Ramirez set the phone back on the hook.

"No answer," she said. "We'll try back later."

"No," I said. "It's Friday afternoon. We'll be going home soon. I can't make it through the weekend without hearing something. Come on, Mrs. R.!"

She shook her head. "We'll try later or on Monday."

My teacher walked out of the room. I turned to Nurse Carol.

"You know the number, don't you?" I asked. "All the good things I've done for you—all the sweeping, cleaning, keeping you company, making your job fun and exciting, how about helping out your favorite student?"

She shook her head.

"Why not?" I asked.

"Mrs. Ramirez would like to talk to the family first to make sure everything is okay," she told me.

"Is something wrong?" I asked.

"Nobody knows yet," she said.

I stared blankly at the ground. *Does no news mean good news or bad news? I hate cancer. I hate it!*

"What are you thinking?" Nurse Carol asked me.

"Nothing," I said. "Nothing at all."

"I can see by the way your eyes are flickering that something is going on in that head of yours," she said. "I'd like to know why you're so upset."

I stared at our school nurse and felt my temperature rise. She was trying to get me to talk about my mother. I stood up and headed toward the door.

"Where are you going?" she asked.

"I've got volleyball practice," I said. "I'm going to be late."

I knew I was being rude, but I didn't care. I needed to get out of that office. Mrs. Ramirez and Nurse Carol had no idea how important it was for me to talk to Peaches. I looked at the girls' locker room door and put all my weight behind my hands. *Bang!* I pushed the door open so hard I almost tore off the hinges. I was strong. Really strong. I rolled up my sleeve, flexed and admired my muscles.

"What are you doing?" I heard a voice call out from behind me.

It was Molly.

"You think you have a muscle?" she asked. "Take a look at this baby."

Molly rolled up her sleeve and held her breath as she flexed. Her face turned beat red.

"You can stop now before you pass out," I said.

She blew all the air out of her. "What do you think?"

"Mine is much bigger."

"Mine has more definition," Molly said.

"Who cares? Strength is all that matters."

"I'm strong," Molly insisted.

"Puh-leze, Mo," I said. "Give it a rest."

"Let's go then," she called out. "Arm-wrestling contest right now."

Molly dropped her bag of books, and I knelt down in front of the locker room bench. Three girls gathered around us, and then Penny walked in the door.

"Watch me crush Molly," I told Penny with a grin.

Penny hustled over and placed her hands on our fists. "One, two, three, go!"

Within three seconds I pinned Molly's hand against the bench. I stood up and flexed in front of my teammates. "With this kind of strength, I should be starting."

My teammates all gave me high fives and smiles. I felt good. I looked at Molly as she stared at the ground dejectedly.

"Keep eating your spinach and you'll get stronger," I said.

She scoffed at me. "Thanks a lot."

I walked over and patted her on the back.

"Would you hurry up?" she said. "We can't be late for practice."

We changed our clothes in the locker room, and then I stopped at the sinks.

"Hurry up, Wil!" Anita said. "Don't be late!"

"And don't rip your shorts," Penny said.

"Would you all just relax?" I said.

They all hustled out of the locker room as I washed my hands.

"Any day now!" Molly screamed.

I took some soap out of the dispenser. "I'm washing my hands!" I yelled back. "Do you know how many germs are spread when people don't wash their hands?"

Nobody answered. I turned off the tap and sprinted out of the locker room. I looked up at the clock when I made it to the gym. I made it by thirteen seconds.

"Hi, Coach Kim!" I said. "I can't wait to practice today!"

"You were almost late," she said as she walked right past me.

"Can I get a little respect?" I muttered. "How about a simple, 'Hi, Wil, how are you today?'"

I almost wanted her to hear me, but she didn't. I really didn't want to be at practice at all that day. I had too much on my mind. We started our warm-up jog around the gym.

"Run harder, Wil!" Coach Kim screamed. "You're doggin' it!"

Okay. Maybe I'm not in the mood today. Did you ever consider for one second what it must be like to be me? Working so hard every day, playing like a champion, putting my body through all of this, and all I get from you is "You're doggin' it?"

I slowed down and jogged as slow as I could.

"This is your last warning," Coach Kim said firmly.

"Come on, Wil," Molly said. "What's wrong with you?"

"Are you all right?" Penny asked.

"She's going to kick you out if you keep it up," Molly warned.

The thought of being tossed from practice raced through my mind.

"Wil!" Coach Kim screamed.

I burst into a full sprint. I worked as hard as I could for the rest of practice. On every play I told myself what a champion I was because no one else did. I looked around and wondered what practice would have been like if I had been asked to leave. *Would anyone care?* When the last whistle blew, I walked slowly off the court. I didn't say much in the locker room after practice or on the way home. I waved goodbye to my friends and headed into my apartment building.

"Wil!" I heard Angel's voice call out.

I turned and smiled. Angel ran up to me. "What's up?" she asked.

"Nothing," I added. I put on a phony smile. "How's soccer and running, Angel-cake?" Angel played soccer and ran cross-country during the same season, which I thought was totally nuts.

"Fine," she said.

"How are the dawgs?" I asked.

Angel stared down at her feet and said, "The dawgs are just fine."

"It might be your plantar fascia or your Achilles," I said. "I looked it up in my anatomy book."

"My feet are fine," she insisted. "Don't sweat it."

"Are you telling me the truth?" I asked.

"Yep," she said with a grin. "I wouldn't lie to the Truth."

I grinned back. "You like my nickname?" I asked.

"It's cool," she said. "How's volleyball?"

I groaned. "I'll take the fifth."

"The fifth?" Angel asked.

"Yeah," I said. "The Fifth Amendment of the Constitution. I don't want to say anything that could incriminate me."

Angel laughed. "Is it that bad?"

"Can I trust you?" I asked.

Angel nodded. I stepped closer to her.

"I almost got kicked out of practice today," I whispered. "I can't stand Coach Kim."

"How many games do you have left?" she asked.

"Two this week coming up and then only one after that."

"Have you been playing much?"

I rolled my eyes. "I wish. Coach Kim doesn't have a clue. She doesn't have any idea of how good I am."

"What about the Brightest Stars competition?" she asked. "How is that going?"

"Fine, except I have to be in it all by myself," I said.

"What?" she said. "What about your partner?"

"Peaches' brother is sick," I said. "She had to go to the hospital with him."

"Oh, no," Angel said. "What's wrong?"

I hesitated. I didn't know if I had the courage to say the word.

"What is it?" she insisted.

"He has cancer," I said. "A brain tumor."

Angel looked up in the sky and closed her eyes as she took a deep breath. I think she was saying a quick prayer.

"What day did you say the Stars competition is?" Angel asked.

"One week from tomorrow at Keller School," I said.

"I don't think I can go," Angel said. "I've got to run."

"That's all right," I said. "We'll videotape it for you so you can watch it later."

Angel grinned, as she jogged down the stairs. I could tell by her careful steps that her feet were bothering her.

"Take care of those dawgs!" I said.

"I will!" she replied.

I called out all the famous artists in alphabetical order as I walked up the stairs. When I reached the top, I screamed, "Picasso!"

"What?" Vicki stared at me after she opened the door.

"Nothin'," I said.

"Your teacher just called," she said.

"Mrs. Ramirez?" I asked.

"Yeah," she said. "That's it. Here's her number."

I took the piece of paper from Vicki's hands and

thanked her. I ran into my room, picked up the phone, and dialed the number on the slip of paper.

"Mrs. R.?"

"Yes," she replied.

"This is Wil."

"I have Peaches' phone number for you," she said.

"Did you talk to her?" I asked.

"Yes," she said. "For a few minutes."

"Is everything all right?"

"The doctors are still doing a lot of tests."

"Can I call?"

"Yes," she said. "But you can't call until tomorrow night after seven."

"I won't," I said. "I promise."

Mrs. Ramirez read me the number, and I wrote it down.

"Wil," she warned. "I hope everything is okay, but the family won't know until tomorrow after the tests are back. Be sure to ask Peaches if she feels like talking."

"I will," I said. "Thanks, Mrs. R. It means a lot to me."

"I know it does," she said. "Call me if you need to talk."

"Okay," I said. I hung up the phone and rewrote the number on a separate sheet of paper just in case I lost the original. I pinned the spare to my bulletin board and put the original in my underwear drawer. Then I turned to the clock.

Twenty-five hours and twenty-two minutes until I could call Peaches.

Chapter 11

Clothes, papers, and junk covered the furniture and tables throughout our apartment. I just couldn't handle the chaos anymore. With everyone sleeping in on a Saturday morning, I rolled out of bed and started cleaning. I began in the kitchen, organizing the food in the refrigerator and stacking a few cans neatly in the pantry. I hand washed and dried all the dishes while reading the list of vocabulary words I had placed on the windowsill. Then I called out greetings and common phrases in French, Spanish, and Italian as I swept the floor. I read my history book while I dusted the living room. When I heard footsteps down the hall, I looked up. It was Blake.

"Hey, B.," I said.

"Hi," he replied. He walked over, turned on the TV, and sat down on the couch.

"Why don't you read something?"

Blake looked at me and shrugged.

"You shouldn't be watching TV so much," I told him. "You should be using your head. Why don't you get a book?"

He shrugged. "I don't know how to read. I'm only four."

"There's no better time to start than today," I said. "Go wake up Lou-Lou and ask her for the alphabet book."

He ran down the hallway with a smile. "I'm going to read! I'm going to read today!"

I finished cleaning up the kitchen and went to the closet. It was time to pull out the vacuum and wake up the entire house. I wanted my father and Vicki to hear how much work I had done. Nobody ever explained to Vicki that housework was a team sport. I flicked the switch on the vacuum and started on the floor. Within seconds all three boys and my sister emerged from their bedroom.

"Here's the book!" Blake screamed over the noise. "Come on! Let's read!"

I held my finger up and shouted, "Wait until I'm finished!"

He nodded. When I finished vacuuming, Lou-Lou had already started reading the book to the boys.

"What letter comes after J?" she asked.

They all looked at each other.

"I've already gone over this," she said. "Come on. You know it. H . . . I . . . J . . ."

"K!" Ricki yelled.

I retreated to my room and started my own session of intense studying. I made up flashcards, outlined difficult essay questions, and flipped through the dictionary to quiz myself on any word my eyes picked out. I wrote all answers three times and then repeated the information aloud. After over an hour I started to break a sweat.

"I am a machine!" I said. "Nobody can stop me!"

Then I looked at my alarm clock. I still had hours before I could talk to Peaches. I flipped the clock around so I wouldn't look at it anymore. I had to study. I had to concentrate.

The phone rang. I heard footsteps down the hall. Louise peeked in my room. "Truth?" she asked.

"Yes," I replied.

"Are you taking calls right now?" she asked.

"Who is it?"

"It's Molly. She wants you to come down to her house and then go to the park."

I picked up the phone and said, "You're such a bad influence on me."

Molly laughed. "I am not!"

"You are. Here I am studying for the biggest competition of my life, and you're asking me to hang out and play some ball. How can you do this to me?"

"Do you want to play or not?" she asked.

"I'll be over in five minutes," I said, giving in.

Lou-Lou escorted me down to the O'Malleys' house. We went straight into the backyard when we heard shouts and laughter. Penny and Rosie were already shooting hoops on the small basket in the corner of the tiny backyard. Molly's brother Frankie and sister Annie chased down Penny's brother Sammy as he ran around cradling a football in his arms. Louise snuck up behind him and tried to tackle him. Sammy shook her off.

"Be strong, Lou!" I said. "Don't let anybody push you around. Go get him!"

She darted after him, and I walked over to my friends.

"Where's Angel?" I asked.

"She's at a cross-country meet," Penny said.

"We need to talk," Molly added. "Let's go into our office."

Our office was the foundation of a fort that Frankie had started to build in a corner of the backyard. The roof wasn't on yet, so it hadn't officially passed our inspection test. But we deemed it safe and crawled through the small door.

"Angel's parents are not getting along," Molly started.

A dreadful moment of silence passed.

"Angel won't talk about it," Rosie added.

"I think we should let her bring it up," I said, thinking about how I'd feel. "That's personal. Maybe she really doesn't want to talk about it."

"She needs somebody," Penny said.

"We'll just keep asking her if everything is okay," Molly suggested. "That way she can talk to us about it if she feels the time is right."

"Don't make a big deal of it," Rosie said. "We don't want to make her feel that she should be ashamed."

"If anybody else starts talking about it, let's just drop it," Penny said firmly. "It's none of our business unless Angel brings it up."

We all sat there and looked at each other.

"How's Peaches' brother?" Molly asked, changing the subject.

"I don't know," I said. "I'm going to talk to her tonight."

"Talking about all this depressing stuff is bringing me down," Penny said. "Let's do something."

"Let's take a visit down to the Drill Sergeant's house," Molly suggested.

"I'm way too tired," I said.

"Come on, Wil," Molly pleaded.

"I thought we declared a truce with him."

I really was not in the mood to test the Sarge and my footspeed. I already had enough on my mind.

"We'll just stop by for a visit," Molly said. "I've got a really good idea."

"Here we go," Penny muttered.

"You're really a bad influence on us," I said. "I'm telling you—you're bad!"

"Relax," Molly said. "You'll like this."

As we walked down Broadway Avenue, Molly jogged ahead of us.

"We need to get the boys," she said.

"What exactly do you have up your sleeve, Mo?"

"We need to make sure the boys are in front of the Drill Sergeant's house at just the right time," she said with a sly smile.

A light bulb flicked on in my head and I grinned. We were going to frame the boys. Molly huddled with us at the corner of Broadway and Woodside and shared the details of her plan.

"Wil and Penny, you get the boys to run over to the corner when we give you the sign," Molly said. "When they get close to you, run for cover."

"Let me get this straight," I said. "You and Rosie are going to ring the bell, and when the Drill Sergeant comes out, he's going to see the boys. One of the oldest tricks in the book."

"That's right," Molly said. "This is ding, dong, ditch and watch the innocent bystanders take the heat."

"J.J., Eddie, and Mike are not going to be happy," Penny warned.

We grinned as we took our places. Molly and Rosie moved closer to the house. We laughed and pointed in the distance.

"You guys have got to see this!" I screamed. "You won't believe it!"

When the boys started jogging over, Rosie sprinted up to the door to perform the classic ding, dong, and ditch. Penny and I started running, and the boys ran faster to catch up with us. We ducked down an alley and hid behind some garbage cans and watched our masterpiece unfold. Just as the boys reached the front of the Sergeant's house, the Sarge opened the door. He spotted Eddie, Mike, and J.J. on the move and jumped into a full sprint. The boys saw him coming toward them, and they started running away.

"It wasn't us!" J.J. screamed. "It was the girls!"

We all laughed hysterically from our hiding spots.

"We could charge admission for this kind of entertainment," I joked.

After a few minutes we snuck down to the park and

took over the courts. Twenty minutes later I looked in the distance and watched the boys storming down the street right toward us.

"Uh-oh," Penny said. "Here they come and they don't look happy."

We kept shooting around as we waited.

"On a scale of one to ten, how mad do you think they are right now?" I asked.

We turned and looked at Eddie's evil glare. J.J. pointed his finger at us and Mike scowled.

"Twelve," everyone said in unison.

"You're gonna pay!" J.J. screamed.

"We didn't even start anything with you!" Eddie said.

All of the Ballplayers laughed. "It was just a little fun," Molly said.

"Where's your sense of humor?" I teased.

"You think it's funny when Carl Lewis is on your heels?" J.J. asked.

"That guy can really run," Mike said.

"Did he catch you?" Rosie asked.

"No," Mike said. "We split in three directions. He followed me, but I lost him in the alley. We're going to get you back for this when you least expect it."

"Oh, yeah," Penny said. "How about you take it out on us on the court."

"You can count on that," J.J. said.

We played for two hours and lost almost every game to the boys.

"It's been fun, ladies," Eddie said sarcastically at the end of the last game. "Maybe you'll think twice about pulling any fast ones on us again."

"Whatever," I said. I headed home so I could enjoy a full night of studying. "See you later."

On the way I stopped by the O'Malleys' and picked up Lou-Lou. Vicki rushed out the door as we ran in.

"Good," she said. "Perfect timing. You'll be in tonight, right?"

I nodded.

"I'm going out," she said as she slipped out the door. "Thanks for watching the kids."

She was out the apartment and down the stairs so fast that I didn't even have a chance to protest. I changed my clothes, washed my hands, and walked into the kitchen. Within minutes I whipped up a pan of macaroni and cheese for all of us. I organized a team cleanup after dinner and gave us a goal.

"Thirty seconds to clear the table," I announced. "Do you think we can do it?"

Ricki, John, Blake, and Louise all nodded eagerly.

"Are you sure we're ready?" I asked. "I need complete concentration and effort."

"We're ready," Louise assured me.

"All right," I said and looked at my watch. "On three. One . . . two . . . three!"

I cheered them on the whole way and shouted out instructions.

"Scrape the dish clean!"

"Wipe up that spot!"

"Rinse, rinse, rinse!"

I checked my watch. "Time is up!"

I looked around and nodded in approval. I ran around and gave everyone a high five. As a reward for their good deeds, I announced that I would pop in a movie.

"Now, you can only watch the movie after you're finished reviewing the alphabet and numbers one to a hundred," I said. "Lou-Lou, you're in charge."

She grinned proudly and sat up straight in her seat. I ducked down the hallway and made myself comfortable at my desk. I turned my alarm clock around and read the time: 6:55 P.M. I had five minutes before I could call Peaches.

When the clock hit seven sharp, I dialed the phone. I knew the long distance call would show up on our phone bill along with all the other information calls, but I didn't care. Vicki couldn't get mad at me. She owed me some cash for baby-sitting, and this would be her form of payment.

"Hello?"

"May I please speak with Peaches?" I asked.

"This is she," Peaches replied.

My nerves tingled. I could hear the sadness in her voice.

"Hi. This is Wil. Is now a bad time to talk?"

"No," Peaches said. "It's all right."

"How is Smooth?"

She paused and then took a deep breath. "We still don't know. The doctors came in today and did all these tests. Then they did some more."

"Did they tell you anything?" I asked.

"No," she said.

"I hate when they do that," I muttered. "They did that when my mother was sick, too."

After the words came out of my mouth, I couldn't believe that I had talked about the forbidden subject.

"Did your mom have to go through chemotherapy?" she asked.

"Yeah," I said. "It was awful."

Peaches didn't say much after that. I just kept talking and talking. The more I spoke, the better I felt.

"Please tell Smooth I said hi and that many people are thinking and praying for him and your family."

"I might be back soon," she said.

"What?"

"If the doctors don't give us some answers soon, we're just coming home," she said. "Smooth keeps telling us how badly he wants to go home."

"Really?"

"Yeah," she said. "And he wants me to be in the competition."

"You don't have to worry if you can't make it," I said. "I think I've got it covered. I hope I do. Maybe I don't. I think I might."

"What do you mean you *think* you've got it covered?" she asked. "You're the smartest person I know."

I didn't know how a person with so much stress and sadness could be telling others how great they were.

"That's the nicest thing anybody's said to me in a long time," I said. "Thanks."

"You're welcome," she said. "Now, will you please stop worrying? I'll call you when I know what we're doing."

When I hung up the phone, I didn't know what to feel. I know it was selfish, but I wanted Peaches to come home and be in the competition with me. I also wanted Peaches home because that meant Smooth would be where he wanted to be. After all the suffering he had been through, he and Peaches needed to be at the competition more than any people in the world.

I rested my head down on my books and fell asleep. When I opened my eyes, I remembered that I was supposed to keep an eye on the kids. I ran out into the living room, but all four of them were asleep on the couch. I walked them one at a time into their room and tucked them into bed. Then I went back to my room and studied for another hour. My father was supposed to come home at midnight. Midnight came and passed without my father walking through the door. I gave up and went to bed. I worried about all of the bad things that could have happened to him, and I started to cry all over again.

Even in my dreams I kept crying over everything. I had a very strange dream that night. I got called into the principal's office for playing the trick on the boys. I walked into the office with the "Principal" sign on the door. My mother was sitting at the desk. I jumped up and down and told her how excited I was that she finally reached her goal.

"You did it!" I said. "You did it. You're the principal!"

My mother looked at me and smiled as she asked me to take a seat. She told me what I did wasn't right, and she gave me a detention. I started to cry again. I had never received a detention in my entire life.

"How can you give me a detention?" I asked. "I'm your daughter!"

"Two detentions!" she said.

I started laughing. It had to be a joke.

"Three detentions!" she added. "And you have to wash dishes every night at home for two weeks."

Then my mother walked over to me and gave me a kiss on the forehead. "Now back to class!" she added.

I woke up early in the morning and was glad to see the glass of orange juice that was on the desk. I sat up and took a sip and thought about my strange dream. I dragged myself out of bed and made myself comfortable at my desk. I looked up at the small picture I had of my mother pinned on my bulletin board.

With or without Peaches, we had to win.

Chapter 12

Before I rushed out the door for school, I tore a piece of paper out of my notebook and grabbed one of Louise's crayons off the counter.

> DAD,
>   I HAVE A VOLLEYBALL MATCH TODAY AT 3 PM. IT'S AT LINCOLN. THEY'RE GIVING AWAY $500 CASH IN BETWEEN GAMES.
>
>   YOUR DAUGHTER,
>   WIL T.

I know, I know, a person with the nickname the Truth shouldn't have made up the part about the money. But I didn't feel bad about it. I read an article in a magazine that said money was the all-time greatest gimmick to get people's attention. This had to work.

I walked into the school that morning with Penny on my right and Molly and Rosie on my left. I stood tall and strutted through the door. I imagined that my friends were the Secret Service and I was the President of the United States.

Mr. Gordon walked up to us and said hello. I reached out my hand. He extended his hand, and I shook it firmly.

"Greetings, Mr. Gordon," I said. "It is a pleasure to be in your school, sir."

Mr. Gordon raised his eyebrows. "Why, thank you, Ms. Thomas."

"You can call me Wil."

"Really?" he replied with a grin.

"I insist."

My friends laughed. "You're weird, Wil," Molly said.

"It's Ms. Truth Thomas to you," I stated firmly.

"Are you nervous about this weekend's Brightest Stars competition?" Mr. Gordon asked.

"Not at all, sir," I said with a straight face. "I'm not one to worry."

"Yeah, right," Penny blurted out.

We continued down the hall and went our separate ways. When my friends left, it was as if somebody had let the air out of me. I moped off through the trenches of the eighth-grade wing feeling alone and unprotected.

"Hey, Wil? Did you do your math homework?" a boy asked.

I shook my head. "Nope."

"Wil," a girl called out. "Can I borrow your science worksheet?"

"Nope," I said.

"I'm not cheating," she insisted. "I just want to look at it for a sec."

"I didn't finish it," I told her.

I wished Peaches were with me. The two of us always stuck together during our daily bouts with peer pressure.

"Wil," Anita called out as she waved me over. "Can you help me for a minute?"

I looked at my teammate and thought of all the times she nailed me with the volleyball during practice.

"Please?" she begged.

I sighed as I trudged over and peeked down at my teammate's notebook.

"I've been up all night and I can't figure out this last equation," she said. "I think I've got the answer. Can you check it for me?"

I sighed in relief. *Finally. Somebody who did her homework!* I took a quick look at her work and nodded. "That's right," I said.

"How'd you do that so fast?" she asked.

I just shrugged and grinned.

"You're so smart!"

"Not really," I said shyly.

I loved playing this little pretend-to-be-humble game. I stared down at the ground and batted my eyelashes.

"You're the smartest person I've ever talked to," Anita stated as her eyes grew wide.

"All right," I said with a slight shrug. "Maybe I am a little on the bright side."

"You are a brain!" Anita said.

I scowled at Anita, put my hand on my hip, and set her straight. "This is a warning. I prefer to be called bright, witty, sharp, and intelligent. Call me a brain again and no more help with your homework."

Anita's face turned red. "Sorry. I didn't think brain was such a bad word."

I took a deep breath and apologized for being so moody. "I'm just under a lot of stress lately," I explained. "I've got a lot on my mind with this competition coming up. And I just can't deal with Coach Kim anymore."

"Hang in there," she said. "Maybe you'll play today."

My teammate's words gave me a sense of hope that I carried with me for the rest of the day. As I was getting changed in the locker room before our game, I imagined that my father had picked up the note and he was on his way. I walked into the gym and spotted Mrs. Ramirez and Nurse Carol. When Mr. Gordon walked in, I jumped up and down.

"What are you all excited about?" Penny asked.

"Everybody is here!" I said. "My dad might even come!"

"Really?" Penny asked.

"Yep!" I said proudly.

Unfortunately it was all downhill from there. Mrs. Ramirez and Nurse Carol only stayed for the first fifteen minutes. Every thirty seconds I looked to the gym door, waiting for my father, but he never came.

I didn't even have the energy to sing my lousy sideline blues song. The only thoughts that entered my mind after the contest was that we had two matches left before the season would finally be over. Then the subject of volleyball would be off limits. It would be swept under the rug and never spoken about again.

"Oh, no!" I gasped as I walked out of the gym. I remembered the note I had left my father. I didn't want him to ask me any questions about my performance. If my father ever mentioned the note, the match, or the volleyball season, I'd tell him that he had his facts messed up and his mind was playing tricks on him again.

No, Dad. I'm not on a volleyball team. Who told you I was?

So much for being called the Truth.

Chapter 13

I rushed in the front door and went straight to the kitchen table. I lifted up all the piles of paper and junk, but I didn't see my note. Dropping to my hands and knees, I looked under the table. A white piece of crumpled paper was stuck under a leg of a chair. I reached out, pulled it toward me, and opened it.

"Yes!"

I ripped it up and threw it in the garbage. Then I called out for Louise and she came running.

"How long do you think it will take us to clean this kitchen?" I asked as I looked at my watch. "I say we can clean this room in eleven minutes, thirty seconds."

She clicked her tongue.

"It's a big study night for me, Lou," I said.

"Every night is a big study night."

"Look, Lou. I'm asking you sister to only sister if I can get a little support around here."

She put her hand on her hip, cocked her head back, wiggled her chin, and stared up at the ceiling. It was scary how much she had picked up from me.

"Please?" I begged.

Lou grabbed the broom and mumbled, "The things I do for you." My sister and I cleaned up the kitchen while Vicki and the boys hung out in the living room. I took a look in the refrigerator and smiled. Vicki had actually gone grocery shopping even though I didn't think she knew where the grocery store was. I took out some cheese, bread, and bacon for my famous Wil Thomas's gourmet grilled-cheese sandwiches.

Within seconds the scrumptious smell of the WTs pulled the boys into the kitchen.

"Can I have some?" Ricki asked.

"Have you read at least three books today?"

He nodded.

"Don't lie to me," I warned.

"I'm not," he said. "I'll go get them and show you!"

Ricki ran away and returned with the books in his hand. "See. I wasn't lying!"

"Okay. Good. Have a seat."

After Louise set the table and I put the sandwiches on the plates, Vicki came in and offered to help.

"I'm finished," I said.

"I was sleeping," she said. "I'm sorry. I would have helped."

"I've got a lot of studying to do tonight. Maybe you can clean up."

She nodded and I told myself to trust her with that one simple responsibility.

"What are you studying for?" Vicki asked.

"A competition for school."

"When is it?"

"Saturday."

"Does your father know about it?" she asked.

I nodded. "I told him last week. He might have forgotten about it."

I guess I should have invited Vicki to the biggest event of my grade-school career. I wanted to tell her how famous this was going to make me. I wanted to warn her about all the phone calls I'd be getting and all the autographs I'd have to give out. But I didn't. I figured if it was important to Vicki and my dad, they would both be there for me.

"I'm going to my sister's this weekend," she said. "Sorry."

I felt an ache in my chest. "That's all right. No big deal." I took my glass of juice and sandwich and stomped off to my room. The phone rang and Louise screamed my name.

"Who is it?" I asked.

"Penny," Louise yelled back.

I stood up and walked down the hall.

"We're coming over to quiz you," Penny said. "We have a whole bunch of questions. What do you say?"

"Cool," I replied with a grin.

"We'll be over in five minutes."

"Wait," I added quickly. I looked around our small apartment and heard all the noise in the other room.

"The house is a mess and all the kids are here. Vicki, too."

"You want to come over to my place instead?" she asked.

"Yeah," I said. "I'll be over in six minutes and thirty seconds."

"I'm timing you. Ready, set . . . go!"

I hung up the phone and ran down the hall. I grabbed a notebook, tucked it under my arm, and told Louise that I'd be back later. I slammed the door right after I said it so she didn't have a chance to beg to go with me. This was my dress rehearsal. I had to be focused. I had to be ready.

"What took you so long?" Molly asked as I stumbled inside Penny's house. "You should have made it in less than six minutes."

"How 'bout you go back to my apartment door and see if you can beat that time?" I added with a grin.

Angel laughed. "Not now," she said. "We've got more important things to think about. Are you ready to rumble?"

I nodded.

"Step into my office," Penny announced.

I looked into Penny's bedroom and saw a chair standing in the middle of the room. A sign with the name TRUTH written on it was pinned to the back of the chair.

"Have a seat, Truth," Molly said as all of my friends took out notecards and huddled around me. "And let the torture begin."

I started to sweat. "You're making me nervous."

"That's the point," Angel said. "This is a gamelike situation. You've got to be ready for Saturday."

The room fell silent. I took a deep breath as the Ballplayers sat in a row on Penny's bed, ready to grill me.

"Judge Rosie Jones will be asking the first question," Penny announced.

Rosie stood up and called out her question. "Who was the first African-American woman in the House of Representatives?"

"Come on, Ro," I said. "I knew that answer in first grade."

"No talking trash to the judges," Penny warned. "Just answer the question."

"Shirley Chisholm," I said. "In 1972 she ran for the presidency of the United States and won ten percent of the Democratic Convention votes."

Rosie plopped down in her seat.

"Next," I said.

Molly stood up and cleared her throat. "Can you name the four terrestrial planets?"

I laughed. "Would somebody at least challenge me? Mercury, Venus, Earth, and Mars."

Penny and Angel each had a shot, but nobody could sink my ship. We played the game for more than an hour, and I gave the correct answer to every question. Molly's face started to turn red. "I'm going to get you on at least one," she vowed. She took out a history book and flipped through it.

"Who was Vice President of the United States in 1861?"

"I know everything about the Abe Lincoln days," I said. "That one is too easy. Most people have a tough time remembering the VPs, but not me!"

"What's the answer then?" she asked.

"Hannibal Hamlin," I said surely.

"That's it," Rosie said and threw her hands in the air. "You win. I give up. How do you remember all this stuff?"

I shrugged. "I'm not really that smart," I said with a grin.

"Oh, don't even start," Molly said. "You're the smartest kid who ever walked down Broadway Avenue. We all know it."

"You're going to win," Penny said.

I crossed my fingers for luck. "I hope so."

"What are you going to wear?" Angel asked.

My mind went blank.

"I don't know," I said. "Peaches and I were going to try and get the same outfits. I forgot all about it."

"Any ideas?" Penny asked.

"Just wear a pair of sweatpants and wear your Broadway shirt," Molly suggested. "Go as a Ballplayer."

"She can't look like she just ran in from off the streets," Penny disagreed. "She has to look like a winner."

"I don't know what to do. I don't have anything." My mind raced back to my uncle Kenny. In high school he won the athlete of the year award. On the night of the annual awards banquet, Uncle Kenny stood outside the back door and didn't go in. He didn't go in and accept his award because he didn't own a suit or tie. All he had was a pair of old worn jeans and a pair of beat-up tennis shoes. He stood outside the door until he heard them call his name. When they did, he turned around and cried all the way home.

"I'll just wear my Lincoln sweatshirt," I said. "Nothing fancy."

"My sister has a dress that would be perfect on you," Angel said.

I shrugged, not knowing if I wanted the dress or if I would fit into it.

"I'll bring it over tomorrow night," Angel told me.

I sat on the bed and didn't say anything. I started to sweat again. Forgetting about one simple thing really threw me. I had to regain my composure. Taking a tissue off of Penny's night stand, I wiped my brow.

"You'll do fine," Angel said. "We're going to be yelling, 'The Truth, the Truth, the Truth is number one!' "

I grinned. "Thanks, Angel-cake."

When I got home, I left my dad a note on the table.

DAD,

I JUST WANTED TO REMIND YOU THAT THE SCHOOL COMPETITION IS SATUR- DAY AT 9 A.M. IN CASE YOU FORGOT. GOOD NIGHT.

LOVE,
WIL T.

I tiptoed into my room and found Louise asleep under my covers. I turned on the night-light and went through my flash cards. I read the newspaper and the W section of the encyclopedia. Then I flipped through the *P* section for Peaches. I missed her. I looked at the clock. It was 11 P.M. I wondered if it was too late to call Mrs. Ramirez. With every second that passed I knew it was getting later and later. A decision had to be made. I flew into the other room and picked up the phone.

"Hi, Mrs. R.," I said. "I'm sorry to call you so late. Have you heard from Peaches?"

"No."

I had to change the subject. "What do I have to wear on Saturday?" I asked.

"Whatever you want," she said.

"Like what?"

"Something that makes you look neat and professional," she answered.

"Something nice?" I asked.

"Yes," she said. "Do you have anything?"

I looked into my bare closet. "Oh, sure. I have a whole bunch of stuff. I'll see you tomorrow, Mrs. R."

"Get some sleep, Wil," she said. "You need a good night's rest two nights before an event."

"Oh. Sorry. I'd better go then."

I hung up the phone and looked at the clock. I wanted to wait up for my father and tell him about the competition so he wouldn't forget. But I didn't have time to wait. I needed sleep.

I held my breath as I tiptoed down the dark hallway all by myself. I flicked off the night-light and crawled into bed next to my sister. I stared into the darkness and listened for my sister's breathing.

The Broadway Ballplayers

I never prayed much, but I did that night. I asked for Smooth to get better and Peaches to get back in town so I didn't have to go through this all by myself.

Even if my father couldn't make it, I knew my mother would be there.

Chapter 14

I walked down the eighth-grade hallway, and my mouth dropped open as I read a row of signs on the wall.

GO WIL!
GO LINCOLN!
THE WIL TO WIN!

I grinned and turned to all of my classmates.

"You really shouldn't have," I said. "Such a fuss over little ol' me?" I grinned sheepishly and batted my eyelashes as I basked in the spotlight.

"We know you love it," Anita said.

My smile faded when I turned and looked into Eddie's beady eyes.

He smiled devilishly. "I really think you're going to win," he said. "I just know it."

I raised my eyebrow suspiciously and asked, "What do you want, Eddie?"

"The answers to the last three questions in math," he mumbled as he looked over his shoulder for teachers. "Please. Pretty please?"

I shook my head.

"I'm going to the competition tomorrow," he told me.

"So that means I should give you the homework?" I asked.

"I support you, you support me," he explained.

I shook my head and waved my hand at Eddie as he blurted out some more nonsense. I turned and walked into my homeroom and greeted my teacher.

"How do you feel?" Mrs. Ramirez asked.

"I'm fine," I replied. "Is there any news from Peaches?"

She shook her head. I flopped down in my seat. The bell rang and everyone hustled into our room for the pledge of allegiance. After Mr. Gordon finished the school schedule and meal of the day, he made one extra-special announcement.

"I would like all of you to make every effort to go to Tucker Park this weekend to cheer on your classmate, Wilma Thomas. She will be representing our school in the Brightest Stars Competition. Please support your school and Wil by attending this very important event."

I could feel the beads of sweat forming on my fore-hand. *A very important event? Is Mr. G. saying it is mandatory for every kid at Lincoln to show up? What if they all do? What if I don't win? Will I be kicked out of school?*

During my classes that day, I didn't think about my schoolwork. I wrote out the most frequently asked competition questions and answers in the margins of my notebooks. I brought my notes with me to the bathroom, lunch, recess, and to all my afternoon classes. At the end of the day Penny asked me the big question. "Are you ready?" she asked.

"For what?" I replied coolly. It was my attempt to downplay the amount of pressure I was under. I couldn't let my friends think I wasn't calm for the Brightest Stars Competition.

"Our game!" Molly said. "Did you forget?"

"Oh, no!" I said in shock. In all the worrying about the stars competition, I'd forgotten about the volleyball game. "I'm losing my mind!"

I started hyperventilating.

"Maybe you should skip the game," Molly suggested.

"No, I made a commitment," I said firmly. "I will finish what I started."

An hour later I wondered why I had been so gung ho about this commitment thing. As I sat on the bench with ice packs on both my knee and ankle, I stared blankly out to the floor. A slippery spot on the floor had put a mild sprain in my ankle and bruise on my knee. Then when I stood up to give my seat to a teammate, I stubbed my toe on the bench and fell to the ground in pain. After the spill, I remained on the ground, hoping the nightmare would end.

"Get up, Wil," Coach Kim said. "You can't play if you're down there."

I stood up and returned to my spot on the bench with a renewed sense of hope. Coach Kim did mention the word *play* to me. I eagerly awaited my chance, but it never came. We won the first two games, which gave us the victory. Both coaches decided to play a third game for fun. As usual, the third game was the one that didn't count. It was a chance for all the players who were terminally ill with the sideline blues to feel important. I had to make it interesting. There had to be some kind of incentive so we would not feel like a bunch of leftovers. I huddled my teammates together and said, "Win this one for the Gipper!"

We all cheered, hooted, and hollered, even though nobody really had any idea who the Gipper was. At that moment all I cared about was that it gave us a reason to unite. After we scored five points in a row, I grinned at the success of my inspirational strategy. Then one of my teammates turned to me and asked, "Who's the Gipper?"

"He's this guy who played football at Notre Dame," I said.

"Why are we playing for him?" she asked.

"It's a legend," I said. "People say it for good luck."

She didn't look convinced.

"Just say it for me," I said.

"So now we're doing this for you?"

"Yeah," I said. "Why not?"

My teammate looked at me and shook her head in disbelief. When we won the game, nobody else asked about the Gipper. Everyone was all smiles in the locker room. Then, once we left the building, I started to think about the rest of the match as I stared out the window of the bus. *This isn't fair. This stinks! How much longer am I going to be able to put up with this?*

Penny nudged me with her elbow. "You all right?"

I tried to open my mouth, but nothing came out.

"Don't be down," she said. "Look at the *bright* side of things. The competition is about here, and you're one of the *brightest* kids in the city. Think about that."

Still down, I said goodbye to all of my friends and turned toward my apartment building. As I walked up the mountain of stairs, I decided that it was time for a Wil Thomas Pep Talk to yours truly.

"Think about tomorrow," I told myself. "The biggest day of your life to date!"

I walked in the front door and gave everybody a high five.

"Hey, hey, what do you say?" Louise said with a grin.

"I say tomorrow is a big day!" I cheered.

I sat down at the table and practiced signing autographs. I tore off sheets of paper and personalized my signatures to my sister and stepbrothers.

"That's going to be worth some money someday," I said confidently.

Then the phone rang. I picked it up.

"Hi, it's Angel. I'm coming over with that dress I told you about."

I paused. "I don't think it's going to fit," I muttered.

"Don't worry," Angel assured me. "It will. I'll be over in five."

I checked my watch as I tried to straighten up the living room in less than five minutes. With ten seconds to spare I heard a knock. I put the broom and dustpan away and hurried to the door. Angel greeted me with a smile as she caught her breath.

"Even with your bad feet, you can still get here faster than most," I said.

Angel winced in pain as she limped inside my apartment. She untucked a plastic bag and a hanger from under her arm.

"Let's go in my room," I said. I didn't want to look like a fool in front of Vicki and the kids if the dress didn't fit. After we both walked into the room, I shut the door. Angel smiled as she unveiled the dress.

"Here it is!" she said. "I can't wait for you to try it on!"

I looked at the long navy dress with short-cut sleeves and pretty white lace. It was so beautiful! Then I looked at the thin waistline.

"I can't fit into that itty bitty waist," I protested. "I'll just wear my Lincoln sweatshirt and a nice pair of pants."

"Try it on," Angel insisted, and she handed me the dress.

I took the dress from her and rested it on my bed. Angel looked away from me as I quickly took off my volleyball clothes and slipped on the dress.

"Okay," I said.

Angel smiled as she hurried behind me and zipped up the zipper.

"It looks great!" she said. "Go look in the mirror."

I stuck my head out the doorway and looked both ways. With the coast clear, I tiptoed to the bathroom, ducked inside, and slammed the door. I took a deep breath and looked into the long mirror hanging on the back of the door. I stared deeper into the mirror, unable to believe that it was me. I looked absolutely stunning. Gorgeous. Beautiful. Elegant.

Bang! Bang! Bang! Three knocks on the door brought me back to earth.

"What are you doing in there?" Louise yelled.

"Nothing." I kept staring into the mirror. This time I saw something about me that I had seen in someone else. I stepped closer to the mirror and saw a dashing smile, full cheeks, and intelligent eyes. I had seen this person before.

I looked just like my mother.

I woke up fifteen minutes early the next morning. Instead of lying in my bed, I got up and headed straight to the bathroom. I spent a few extra minutes in the shower and the rest of my time putting the finishing touches on my hair. Then I put on what I called my "evening gown." I heard a gentle knock on the door, so I opened it. My father paused as he looked at me in my dress and said, "You look nice."

"Thanks," I muttered, a bit disappointed that he didn't use a stronger adjective than *nice.* "Are you coming to the competition?"

When he shook his head, my knees felt weak. My bottom lip began to quiver.

"I didn't give my boss enough notice," my father said. "He needs me today for a double shift. I might get promoted this week."

I didn't have the strength to speak.

"I'm sorry," he said. "I know it's important to you."

I mustered some courage and shrugged. "It's no big deal," I said, trying to sound like I didn't care.

"Is Louise going with you?" he asked.

"The O'Malleys are taking her," I explained. "I have to go early with my teacher."

My father's tired eyes stared at the ground. He truly felt bad.

"Don't worry," I said.

"I brought you home a few bottles of orange juice to take with you," he offered.

I gave my father a big smile in hopes of making him feel better. Just before he turned to go down the hallway and out the door, my father stopped and looked at me again. "You look just like your mother," he said softly. The room fell silent. "I bet she is really proud of you right now."

After he shut the door, the tears gushed out of me. It was one thing for me to notice that maybe I slightly resembled my mother, but it hurt me so much to hear the words from my father. He never talked about her. *Why did he have to tell me this now?* I started to cry harder. I looked in the mirror as I was crying and saw how miserable and pathetic I looked. Taking a deep breath, I told myself to stop.

The tears came and went for the next few minutes. When Louise walked down the hall and sat down at the kitchen table, I hid my eyes from her.

"Molly is coming to get you in one hour," I said. "Make sure you're ready and don't forget to thank the O'Malleys for taking you."

I poured a bowl of cereal for my sister and then washed my dishes. I sat in the living room and read over my notes as I waited for Mrs. Ramirez. When a car horn blared, I jumped. Lou-Lou ran to the window and looked down onto the street.

"She's here!" she said.

I grabbed my bag and hustled to the door. My sister ran up to me and handed me a card.

"Read it!" she said.

I opened it up and it read:

THE TRUTH WILL WIN! I LOVE YOU!

I smiled at how clever she was. I looked at the words I LOVE YOU! and felt the tears return. Then the horn blared again. "Later, Lou!" I called out.

"Go get 'em, Truth!"

I started running down the steps as fast as I could. I imagined seeing Peaches in the front seat of Mrs. Ramirez's car. I grinned at the thought of having my teammate with me and knowing that Peaches and Smooth were all right. When I arrived at the car, I realized that Peaches wasn't there.

"I don't want to go," I said as I backpedaled.

Then I felt arms on my shoulders. "Wil!" Mrs. Ramirez said. "Wil! What's wrong?"

"I can't do this. Nobody has ever won the competition alone. How am I supposed to win against two people? I can't do this by myself!"

"You have the mind of a dozen people put together," she said.

I kept shaking my head. I thought of all the people at school counting on me. I looked down at the card from Louise I had in my hand.

"Do you think I would have worked this hard if I didn't believe you could do it?" my teacher told me. "You'll be the smartest kid in the room. You have more knowledge and facts in your head than most adults. You're brilliant!"

I lifted my eyes up and looked at my teacher. "Do you really think so?"

She nodded. "I do. Now will you please get into the car."

"All right. If you insist. But promise me one thing."

"What?" she asked.

"If people ask you if I was nervous or scared, don't tell them about what just happened," I said.

"All right," she agreed. "I promise."

"Good," I said and I smiled at my teacher. After putting up with me for so long, Mrs. R. deserved a reward. But I didn't have any flowers. I didn't even make her a card, I thought quickly.

"When they make a movie about me," I said, "I'll be sure that they make you a main character."

My teacher looked at me and smiled.

"Let's just worry about winning this competition first," she said.

Chapter 15

Rows of tables with numbers and school names covered the floor of Tucker Park's indoor gymnasium. Some students pressed their hands against their foreheads as they sat reading over their notes. Others paced up and down the rows, moving their lips and staring down at the floor. Whispered words and quiet laughter spread softly around the room.

"Are you all right?" Mrs. Ramirez whispered to me.

"Yep," I said, nodding my head repeatedly. "Don't sweat it, Mrs. R."

As I looked at all the girls in their sharp dresses and the boys in their spiffy jackets and ties, I wondered if anyone else had to borrow their clothes for the event. My eyes moved up to the ceiling and stopped on the colorful banners.

THE CITY'S BRIGHTEST STARS
Youth who make a difference

Butterflies fluttered in my stomach. When I felt the beads of sweat sliding down my forehead, I searched frantically in my bag.

"How could I forget my tissue?" I said. "What is wrong with me? How can I be so stupid?"

Mrs. Ramirez reached into her purse. She pulled out a fresh pack of tissues and handed them to me. "I brought them just for you."

"I don't know what I would do without you, Mrs. R.," I said. "If I had some money, I'd buy you a cool car or an expensive vacation to anywhere you want to go."

My teacher smiled and rested her hand on my shoulder. "I know you would, Wil. Do you have to use the rest room?"

"I should stay and study like everyone else," I said. "How much time do we have?"

"Thirty minutes until the first round," she said. "Are you sure you don't need to use the rest room?"

I thought about my tendency to have emergencies at the worst possible situations. "Yeah," I said. "I'd better go. But you gotta come to the bathroom with me." I tugged on my teacher's arm.

"Why?" she asked.

"I had this bad dream once," I said.

"About what?"

"It's going to sound crazy," I began. "But in my dream I walked into the wrong locker room and saw all the judges in their underwear."

Mrs. Ramirez burst out laughing.

"It's not funny," I protested. "They disqualified me because I saw them in their underwear!"

"So you want me to check out the rest room first?" Mrs. R asked.

"Would you do that for me?"

She walked down the hallway shaking her head. She stopped in front of the women's room sign and pushed the door open. I waited outside until she returned. A few seconds passed, and she walked out the door. Mrs. Ramirez looked me in the eye and said, "The coast is clear."

"Thanks!"

I rushed in and out of the bathroom and then returned to Mrs. R. in the hallway. "Time to study!" I said.

She shook her head. "Come in this room with me."

We ducked into a small coaches' office. My teacher sat down and then pointed to the open chair. "I want you to close your eyes," she said as I took my seat.

I raised my eyebrow at my teacher. "What?"

"Trust me, Truth," she assured me. "You need to relax."

"I need to study like everyone else!" I blurted out.

"Do this for me," she said.

I shook my head.

"I want you to close your eyes and think of the most relaxing place you've ever been," my teacher said.

I sighed loudly as I closed my eyes. I hadn't been to many relaxing places or great vacation resorts. The only thing that I could think of was how much I loved to swim in the city pool. Just for fun, I imagined what it would feel like if I was floating in the ocean. I started to block out all the words from my teacher and focused on the water that carried me. The waves lifted me as I floated gently and safely along the water's surface. The sunlight warmed the blue water, and I stayed on top of the water like a baby with bright orange swimmies on her arms.

"Wake up, Wil!" Mrs. R. said loudly. "Wake up!"

I whipped my head up from off the desk and sat up straight.

"What happened?" I blurted out.

"You fell asleep," she said.

"I did what you asked," I explained.

"Just remember how calm you were when you get out there for the competition," she said.

"Okay," I said. "I can do that. But please make sure I don't fall asleep."

As I walked out to the main room, the increased noise level hit me hard. The bustling crowd had finally arrived. I grinned as I walked past Mr. Gordon and gave Molly, Penny, and Rosie high fives. I looked down at Lou-Lou and winked. Anita and Samantha pushed through the crowd, whispered my name, and waved. I looked to my right and saw Nurse Carol. Next to her stood J.J. and Eddie.

Eddie waved and yelled from across the quiet room, "I told you I'd be here!"

"Are you getting extra credit for this?" I asked, shaking my head.

Then I bit my lip and felt shots of pain and tightness in my stomach.

"I wish Peaches were here," I told my teacher.

Mrs. Ramirez looked past me and her eyes grew wide. "It looks like your wish just came true," she said. "Look!"

I looked over my shoulder and instantly started screaming. I bumped into at least ten people as I sprinted across the room.

"You're here!" I shouted. "You're here!"

I ran up to Peaches McCool and gave her the biggest, tightest hug I had ever given anyone. Then I looked down at Smooth, who was in a wheelchair in front of his sister. When he gave me the thumbs-up sign, a chill shot up my spine.

"I am so glad to see you!" I said, grabbing his hands. "Thank you for coming! I can't do this without you!"

By this time all the commotion had caused everyone to turn and watch me carry on.

"Come on, Wil," Peaches said quietly to me. "We came here to win."

I settled down and strutted off to our table with Peaches at my side. Molly and Penny wheeled Smooth up to the front row. The judges took their seats and I held my breath. I imagined them in their underwear and started to laugh.

"Shhh!" Peaches said.

"Finally the moment you've all been waiting for is here," a judge with black-rimmed glasses said, staring right at me. I pushed up my glasses, sat up straight, and tried to look intelligent. "Let the games begin!"

Four assistants handed out the individual multiple choice test. Thirty-five minutes later we handed it back in. After a few minutes the judges posted the combined scores. When the judge placed the LINCOLN sign under the first-place spot, our entire cheering section went crazy.

"Lincoln is number one!" Eddie screamed.

"Go, Wil, go, Peaches!" Lou-Lou called out.

I gave Peaches a hug. I still couldn't believe that she had come back. I felt so good for her family. So happy for Smooth.

"We're gonna win," I said emphatically. "It's our destiny."

Round two were the team essays. I looked quickly at our paper and saw one of my strongest subjects: WOMEN'S SUFFRAGE. I grinned and twisted my hands together. We read the question twice together and then picked it apart. Twenty minutes later Peaches finished the last sentence, and we handed in our paper. Below our school name she signed it Peaches M. and I signed it Truth T. As we walked across the room for our break, I talked to Peaches. "When did you get back in town?"

"Four o'clock this morning," she said.

"That late?" I gasped. "And you still came?"

"I wanted to be here," she told me.

"How is Smooth?"

"He's much better," she said. "But the doctor said to be prepared for things to get bad again."

My bottom lip began to quiver. I remembered the slumps my mother had gone through.

"All Smooth talked about on the way home was being here," Peaches said.

My eyes filled with happy tears as I thought about how much this competition meant to all of us. Peaches, Smooth, me, and my mother. Then a judge stepped up to the microphone.

"Winners for the second round are Peaches and Truth from Lincoln!" the judge announced.

We hurried back to our tables and waited as the judges called us up for the speed round. I looked around at my smiling friends and noticed there wasn't an empty seat in the house. I looked down at Smooth, and he gave me another thumbs-up sign.

Peaches and I took our spots at the front of the room. I took a long look at the big red buttons we had to push when we knew the answer to the question. I hit it once just for practice. *BZZZ!* The noise was so loud I almost fell over. The entire room laughed at me. I didn't think it was funny, but I smiled anyway.

One by one the judges called out the subjects: U.S. Presidents, The Solar System, Words that Begin with the Letter Q, World Wars, Sports, and Famous Places. I looked at Mrs. R. and winked.

"We got this covered," I whispered to Peaches.

My teammate and I dominated every single subject. We answered the questions so fast that the other team threw their hands up in the air and started to bicker with one another. Peaches and I grinned and exchanged high fives. I pointed to the crowd at the end of each round. They screamed out for us.

"Teach 'em, Peach!"

"The Wil to win!"

Surely it would only be seconds before they would be

whipping out their pens and pieces of paper for our autographs. I glanced around the room hoping to spot the television cameras and news anchors. None were in sight. *Must be on their way.* I slicked back my hair and cleared my throat as the judge called out the last question for the day.

"What is the name of the street in New York City famous for its great theater?"

I dove on the red button. After it sounded, I screamed out, "Broadway!"

The Ballplayers rushed the stage and almost tackled me. After I hugged Peaches, I broke from my huddle of friends and ran into the crowd to find Smooth. Peaches and I both hugged him and screamed, "We won! We won!"

Lou rushed up to me and clung so hard to my waist that I thought she'd have to accept the award with me. After I peeled my sister off, Mrs. Ramirez grabbed me by the shoulders and led me back to the front. "You're representing your school!" she said firmly. "Win like a champion!"

"Sorry," I said. "I just got so excited!"

As we hustled back up to our spots, we walked past the trophy table. My heart stopped as I looked at the biggest and most beautiful trophy I had ever seen in my entire life.

"That's ours?" Peaches said in disbelief.

Mrs. Ramirez nodded proudly. Tears welled in my eyes. All I could do was smile at Peaches. Her tired eyes grinned back at me. I looked across the room and smiled at Smooth. His mother stood behind him, and she waved at me. My heart ached as I waved back.

I lost my breath for a quick second. The moment slipped away as I thought about the two people I wanted in the room.

"Truth! Truth!" a soft voice called out.

Lou-Lou ran up to me and gave me another hug. A chill shot up my spine. I closed my eyes, and took a deep breath.

My heart ached for my father. But slowly the pain faded as the colors behind my closed eyes imagined my mother standing right before me. She clapped, cheered, and told everyone, "That's my baby girl!"

I opened my eyes and she was gone.

Chapter 16

On the way home I stared blankly out the car window. "Are you all right?" Mrs. Ramirez asked.

I shrugged and said thanks as the car came to a stop. Mrs. Ramirez didn't press me any further. She waved goodbye as she watched Lou-Lou and me walk to our apartment building.

"Bring the trophy to school on Monday so Peaches can take it home," Mrs. Ramirez yelled. "Don't forget!"

I forced a smile and waved goodbye. I carried our heavy trophy as Lou-Lou and I walked in the lobby door and up the stairs. I looked at the trophy and tried to convince myself that it was the perfect ending. But it wasn't. My father had missed his chance to see his daughter as a champion. I was the best of the best, the brightest of the brightest, and he didn't even know it. I belted out another verse of my least favorite song.

> *I got the blues.*
> *Oh, I got the blues.*
> *Oh, oh, oh, I got the bluest blues.*
> *Oh, oh, oh, oh . . .*

"Stop!" Louise screamed as she pressed her hands against her ears. "That's bad. Really bad!"

I quit singing as I walked through the front door of our apartment. I decided that I would try and relive the day by explaining my great victory question by question, heartbeat to heartbeat, to my father. I pushed open the door and called out, "Dad! Dad?"

There was no answer. Piles of toys, papers, and junk covered the floor. I cringed at the thought of what was in the kitchen sink.

"Nobody's home," Lou-Lou said.

I set the trophy down right in front of the door so the next person who walked through would trip over it and take notice. I made a pot of macaroni and cheese and we sat down together at the table for dinner.

After dinner, Louise asked, "You want to go to the park?"

I agreed, and for a solid hour I joined my friends for a game of football on the sandlot while Louise played on the swings. After throwing five awesome blocks on Eddie and J.J., I announced to the crowd, "I am the best offensive linewoman in the history of Anderson Park." I flexed for the crowd.

"You go, Truth!" Molly called out. Everyone laughed. I didn't want my day of glory to end.

That night I tried my best to stay awake until my father came home, but all the excitement caught up to me, and I fell asleep reading the business section of the newspaper. I slept until late the next morning. When I woke up, I went into my father's bedroom. He was gone.

"He had to go back to work," Vicki told me.

"When will he be home?"

"Maybe tonight," she replied. "He wanted me to tell you he is so proud of you for winning the competition. He can't wait to hear all about it."

I stared at the floor and walked out of the room. I figured that by the time we actually caught up with each other, my father would have forgotten the Brightest Stars Competition. I walked out into the living room and sat at the kitchen table. The room felt empty.

"Where's my trophy?" I asked the boys.

"We don't know," John said.

I looked by the door and in every closet. Then I searched in my bedroom and the pantry.

"Where is it?" I called out.

Louise ran in my room and said, "I can't find it, either."

I went into the living room and started yelling at the boys.

"Which one of you took my trophy?"

All three boys sat there shaking their heads.

"We didn't do anything to it!" Ricki said.

When Vicki said she had no idea where it was, either, I ran down to the park and asked everyone if they had seen the missing hardware. They all shook their heads.

"Somebody snuck in my house last night and took my most valuable possession!" I exclaimed. "What am I going to tell Mrs. R. and Peaches? I'll be banned from Lincoln School."

I marched home and told Vicki that I was taking matters into my own hands and notifying the local authorities.

"No, you're not," she said. "It's around here somewhere. Ask your father when he comes home."

"When will he be back?" I asked.

"Late tonight," she said.

"If that trophy doesn't show up in twenty-four hours, I'm calling the police."

Chapter 17

When the trophy didn't show up the next morning, I briefly considered playing sick, but packed up my bag and headed out the door instead. When I walked into the front door of Lincoln School, I was still holding my head down in shame.

"Truth," a deep voice called out. "Why the sad face?"

I looked up. It was Mr. Gordon. I stared down at the floor again.

"Somebody stole the trophy," I said as I fought back tears.

"Are you sure?" he asked.

"I'm afraid so, Mr. G. Somebody walked into my apartment and took it. I'm not going to be able to face Peaches and Mrs. R. I should have been more responsible."

"Before you get too upset, why don't you ask around and give it some time to turn up?" he suggested.

"I already asked everyone," I said. "It's hopeless."

"Never let go of hope," he told me.

I told Mrs. Ramirez what had happened, and she didn't think the trophy had been stolen, either.

"Ask around," she said. "It will pop up."

"What, did someone take it for kicks?" I blurted out. "Are they running around the city right now bragging to people about how they were the brightest stars of the city? People are sick. Really sick."

"You keep up that attitude and you'll never get it back," she warned.

I took out a sheet of paper and slammed it on my desk. I picked up a marker and drew a sign, made some photocopies, and posted them around school.

MISSING TROPHY
Description: Gold, black, brown, totally
    beautiful.
Return to: Wil Thomas, 1100 Broadway
    Ave. Apt. 65
REWARD: $50 No questions asked.

"You don't have fifty dollars," Molly said as she looked over my shoulder.

"No kiddin', Mo," I said. "I'll pay in installments."

"In what?" she asked.

"A little bit at a time," I explained.

"That could take years," Penny said.

By the end of the day I wanted to call off the search,

go home, and go back to bed. But we had our last volleyball game of the season to play.

"Hurry up, Wil!" Coach Kim yelled at me in the locker room. "Don't be late!"

I put a brace on each knee and wrapped a bandage around my bad ankle. I took a roll of tape out of Anita's locker and taped up three of my fingers.

"What are you doing?" Molly asked.

"Do you always have to be so nosy?" I shot back.

"When you're walking around like a mummy I do," Molly said. "What's with all the bandages?"

"I'm not hurting myself anymore," I said. "I've had enough injuries this season already."

"Well, you'd better hurry up, or Coach Kim will have us all running for being late," she said.

"So? I don't care."

"Oh, yeah?" Molly asked. "Well, I do!"

She grabbed me by the arm and dragged me into the gym. My body ached just thinking about going through warm-ups. I looked at the wooden bench, walked over to it, and had a seat.

"What are you doing?" Penny demanded. "We've got to warm up!"

"Why?" I asked. "I'm not going to play."

"Come on, Wil."

"I've had a bad day," I said. "I'm just not in the mood."

Penny shook her head. "For somebody so smart, you can really be thick-headed sometimes. Coach Kim is going to be screaming at you in about five seconds," she warned.

I looked across the gym and my eyes stopped when

something caught my attention. A chill shot up my spine, and I rose from the bench. My father stood in the doorway. His eyes scanned the gym until he spotted me. I jumped up and down and waved. "Hey, Dad!" I screamed. "Over here!"

When he smiled, I jogged onto the court and ran through warm-ups like a champion. My teammates cheered for me, "Go, Truth! Go, Truth!"

Coach Kim looked at me in disbelief. "What has gotten into you all of a sudden?"

"Can I please play today?" I begged. "It's so important to me."

She took a deep breath. "No foolin' around on the bench," she began. "And no singing that song of yours. Cheer for your teammates and be ready."

I nodded and started hollering immediately. I ran around and high-fived everyone. I screamed our team cheer louder than ever before. I glanced over at my dad. He was smiling. I jogged out on the floor with the starters.

"Wil," Coach Kim called out. "Not yet!"

I moped back to my spot on the bench. I glanced at my father again, hoping he wasn't too disappointed that I wasn't a starter.

Halfway through the game, Coach Kim called out my name and I almost tackled the ref while running onto the floor. The ref made me come back to the sideline and check in appropriately with my hand raised, standing facing my teammate. As soon as I crossed the line, I screamed.

"Spike 'em, beat 'em, make 'em eat 'em, dig it, yeah!" I

called out as I high-fived Mo, Penny, and Anita. I looked good, I felt good. I was so ready to shine.

I danced around in my spot and focused on every second of play. I bumped the ball three times, dished three awesome sets, and spiked the ball for the final point of the game. The crowd roared. I looked over at my father and he smiled.

I pinched myself on the arm just to make sure I wasn't dreaming. Coach Kim even let me play for half of the second game. I made a bad mistake on one play, but she kept me in for a while. Three plays later she subbed me out. As I passed the bench, Coach Kim stopped me and patted me on my sweaty head.

"Way to play, Truth!" she said.

I grinned as I took off my glasses and wiped the sweat from my eyes. I looked at my father again. The action in the game had swept his attention away from his daughter. I kept watching him as he twitched in his seat, cheering on my friends, rooting for the cause. My heart melted in my chest.

Later when Coach Kim started me for the dreaded "doesn't count" third game, I sprinted on the floor. "Let's go, Lincoln!" I cheered.

We won the third game. I had three spikes, six bumps, and four sets. As we walked off the court, I felt the butterflies in my stomach. I couldn't stop smiling.

"This is the best day of my life," I told Penny.

She patted me on the back as I walked over to my father. He greeted me with a smile and said quietly, "Good job."

I shrugged coolly and said, "I played okay."

"Mrs. Ramirez told me how well you did at the Brightest Stars Competition," he told me. "I can't wait to hear all about it."

"It was so cool," I began. My heart started to race. "Peaches and I ran the show. You remember Peaches, right? It all started when I thought I was going to have to compete all by myself—"

"Why don't you tell me all about it on the way home," he suggested. "Go get your things, and we'll go out and get something to eat."

Sweat continued to pour down my face as I ran into the locker room.

"I'm going out to eat with my dad!" I told everyone. Nobody said anything so I told them again. "My dad's here."

Penny and Molly reached out and gave me a high five.

"Sweet!" Penny said.

I rushed out into the parking lot and opened the door to my father's beat-up old truck. I gasped when I saw what was sitting on the front seat.

"Our trophy!" I exclaimed. "I thought somebody stole it! I was going to call the police!"

"I'm sorry," he said. "I should have told you. I took it to work to show everyone. My boss put it in the front window, and I forgot to pick it up when I left last night."

I felt the tears well in my eyes. "You did?"

He nodded. "I'm really proud of you," he added.

My father and I talked and joked during dinner. Actually, I was the one doing most of the talking and joking. My father just sat there shaking his head at me in amazement.

"Are you having a good time?" I asked.

"I'm having a great time." He sat across the table and stared at me. "Your mother is proud of you. I know she is."

The chill that shot up my spine left me speechless.

"She's up there looking down at us, saying what a great daughter she has," he went on. "*Two* great daughters."

I exhaled slowly and looked my father in the eyes. "I know she was watching me at the competition," I said softly. "I could feel her there."

"She was so proud," he said surely.

All my worries and fears drifted away. After all the years of hesitation and doubt, the words my father said at that moment had set me free.

"Can we talk about Mama every now and then?" I asked.

He nodded. "Whenever you want."

"And whenever you want to talk, go ahead," I said eagerly. "Everybody knows how much I love to talk. I'm really quite good at it."

"You're just like your mother, " he added with a grin.

We finished eating and went home to a house full of screaming kids and Vicki. I set the trophy on the kitchen table.

"Where'd you find it?" Lou-Lou asked.

"Dad had it," I said, gushing with pride. "He took it into work to show everyone."

I invited Louise into my room and let her sit at my desk to do her homework. Then I cleaned the bathroom and organized my bedroom before I cracked open the books. When my father left for work again, he came in and said goodbye.

"When will you be home?" I asked.

"Five in the morning," he answered.

I wanted so badly to tell him how he made that day the best day of my life. But I couldn't. I didn't want him to feel bad for all the games he had missed.

"Thanks, Dad," I said. "I'll see you tomorrow."

I sat up late that night. I couldn't sleep as my mind filled with worry about my father not coming home. I thought of all the dangerous equipment at work and the long ride home. *Please, please come home!*

Later, after I had finally fallen asleep, I felt a gentle kiss on my forehead. I rolled over and wondered if I had been dreaming. From a stream of light pouring through the window, I could see something sitting on my nightstand. It was a cup.

I sat up with a smile and raised the cup to my mouth. It was the smoothest, coolest, most delicious glass of orange juice that I had ever tasted.

About the Author

Sometimes my mom comes out in the driveway with us and takes a few shots at our old hoop. She bends her knees, cocks the ball under her chin, and bangs it as hard as she can against the backboard. My brothers and sister and I all look at each other and laugh.

"Don't laugh!" she tells us. "Nobody ever taught me how to play."

The girls in her grade school played three-on-three basketball. Some players on the team weren't allowed to cross half court because people in athletics didn't think girls were strong enough to play in a full game. In high school there weren't any girls' teams. With little else to keep her busy, my mother worked a bunch of odd jobs to pay her way through high school and nursing school. After picking one job out on a limited list of professions for women—nurse, teacher, or housewife—my mom got married and had four kids. For years she worked double shifts taking care of the sick and injured, and then she came home and took care of us.

I've seen my mother touch the hands of many strangers and make them smile. I've seen her come home from double shifts for years and the little she gets in return. I sometimes wonder what kind of athlete my mother would have been and how it would have changed her life if she had had a chance to play sports. I imagined that if we were the same age and out at the park playing ball that I would recognize my mother's strength and put her on my team.

After all the years of being able to play so many sports, it breaks my heart to know that no one ever gave her a chance. What amazes me most is that instead of feeling sorry for missed opportunities, she has dedicated her life to giving both her sons and daughters every chance to excel. Thanks to my mom, instead of being told that I could only pick one of three professions, my sister and I proudly juggle several that didn't make the list for women back then, all at the same time.

My dad always tells us how he could jump so high he could get his elbows on the rim. We don't believe him, but we let him tell his stories anyway.

When we were kids, my father came home from work around five-thirty P.M. every night, and we sat down and had dinner. After we ate and cleared the table, we then ran off to our different activities and sports. My dad coached most of our teams. When he started coaching my fourth-grade softball team and saw the terrible fields we played on, the first thing he did was run for league president. After he won, he took almost every tool, rake, and shovel out of our shed and brought it up to the fields. He plowed and raked and planted grass. Other people in the community joined him, and together they built a concession stand. I went up to the fields last year to watch the girls in my neighborhood play ball, and I took one long look at the beautiful fields and knew the person who made it possible.

Sometimes when my mother and father go to watch us play ball, they cheer very loudly. I have no idea what my mom is yelling sometimes, and I just shake my head at how my dad jumps around in his seat. Now instead of getting embarrassed, I just shake my head and laugh. After all the time they have put in to give us a chance, our parents deserve to have some fun.

The way I live my life has everything to do with the people who raised me. Thanks to them, in your hands is my fourth book.